SHADOWLANDS SECTOR

ONE

MILA YOUNG

Shadowlands Sector

MILA YOUNG

Shadowlands Sector © Copyright 2020 Mila Young
Cover art by TakeCover Designs

All rights reserved under the International and Pan-American Copyright Conventions. No part of this book may be reproduced or transmitted in any form or by any means, electronic or mechanical, including photocopying, recording, or by any information storage and retrieval system, without permission in writing from the publisher/author.

This is a work of fiction. Names, places, characters and incidents are either the product of the author's imagination or are used fictitiously, and any resemblance to any actual persons, living or dead, organizations, events or locales is entirely coincidental.

Warning: the unauthorized reproduction or distribution of this copyrighted work is illegal. Criminal copyright infringement, including infringement without monetary gain, is investigated by the FBI and is punishable by up to 5 years in prison and a fine of $250,000.

FOREWORD

In Shadowlands Sector, I returned to one of my favorite tales to write...fated mate wolf shifter romances.

I loved writing this book so much, and like all of my books, I always put my own spin on legends and myths.

Have a load of fun getting to know Meira and her three Alphas.

Love XOX
Mila

CONTENTS

Shadowlands Sector — ix

Prologue	1
Chapter 1	13
Chapter 2	27
Chapter 3	39
Chapter 4	52
Chapter 5	66
Chapter 6	77
Chapter 7	93
Chapter 8	108
Chapter 9	128
Chapter 10	140
Chapter 11	153
Chapter 12	174
Chapter 13	198
Chapter 14	221
Chapter 15	229
About Mila Young	249

SHADOWLANDS SECTOR

They call me an outcast, weak.

I've fought my whole life for survival, running from an attack on my family I ended up hiding with the Ash Wolves. This one move might be my biggest mistake of all. And I'm the queen of mistakes…

I let them believe I'm broken, let them believe the lies. I let them believe anything they want…as long as it isn't the truth.

There's a monster inside me, one made of teeth and claws and terrifying need. I swallow it down, hiding under the pretense of being normal. But I'm not normal. I'm anything but.

Bonding is the only thing that will save us—me

and the Ash pack. Only I need someone strong enough to fight the darkness inside me...and savage enough to stay.

Will the three ruthless alphas help me...when they find out the truth of what I am?

PROLOGUE

The creak of the door alerts me to someone entering my room.

"Mama?" I roll over in bed expectedly.

But it's Jaine, our neighbor. She rushes to me with wild hazel eyes and messy blonde hair, still in her blue nightgown with patches. Her face is pale, her breaths shallow and raspy. I remember the blood and tears drenching her cheeks when she first came to our settlement after the Shadow Monsters killed her family. It still scares me to remember the fear on her face… and now, she has the same look as she hurries into my room.

The hairs on the back of my neck lift, and I draw my blanket to my chest, a whimper falling from my lips. "What's going on?"

"Meira, sweetie," she whispers, breathing heavily. She is a bit younger than Mama, but already looks out for me. "Death stalks the day. We must be swift and silent now." She chokes on her fast words as tears thread down her cheeks. There's a glint in Jaine's eyes, a window revealing a glimpse of her wolf lingering just below the surface. Her fear thickens the air in my room.

I shuffle to sit upright in bed, straightening my shoulders. "Where is Mama?" The morning light drenches my small room, and silhouettes darting past my windows outside. Their shadows are a frightening puppet show playing out across my drawn curtains.

They move fast.

There are too many of them. We're made up of a dozen females hiding in this settlement from the danger outside. The ten-foot metal fences lined with barbed wire have always kept them out.

"Jaine, what's going on?"

"The creatures are here." She glances over her shoulder to the ajar door. "You need to hide."

A chill fills my body. I hate the Shadow Monsters. I shiver, wrapping my arms around my pajama top and pants. We've been on the run from the creatures before, then Mama and I found this place. Our refuge. Or so I thought.

"I have to find Mama," I whisper.

But Jaine never answers me. She just snatches my arm and yanks me out of bed.

Pain flares through my limbs from the sickness I've suffered since birth. I wince as a pain, resembling claws, drags over my flesh. Mama insists it's related to my wolf side trying to come out. I'm already fourteen and still haven't experienced my first transformation. I shouldn't be alive as a result, but Mama says I'm her miracle girl. For years we've fled the wolves who will have killed me for what I am and we joined other random female settlements to keep me safe. Mama lies to the other women and says I'm only eleven and not at puberty yet so they won't want to kill me. I'm thin and look young for my age. Up to now, we've survived.

"Let's be swift and silent, Meira. Repeat those words in your mind."

My stomach hurts so bad. My gaze swings to the windows, at the commotion outside. Someone screams, and I cringe, grasping on to Jaine's arm. Why isn't Mama coming to get me? Where's everyone else?

This is a safe haven. This is our home.

But Mama was wrong. The Shadow Monsters broke in like they always do.

Jaine leans down, gripping my shoulders, and looks me in the eyes. "Repeat the words: swift and silent. Over and over."

Tears well in my eyes. One year of peace. That is all we've been granted, and now the demons are at our doorstep again.

Jaine takes my wrist, and we duck low as we hurry out of my bedroom and down the hall. She quietly opens the small cupboard door in the hallway where we keep brooms and winter boots. It's where Mama made me practice hiding until I could find it blindfolded. There's a lock on the inside of the door too.

"Swift and silent, baby girl, okay?" Jaine's voice is panicked and shaky.

I stumble into the hiding spot and spin to face her. My heart pounds in my ears. "I'm scared."

An explosive crash comes from somewhere in the background, rattling the whole house. Jaine shuts the door hastily, and darkness swallows me. With shaky fingers, I draw the metal lock into place and back away until my heels hit a bucket.

Huddling down in the corner amid threadbare clothing, I hug my knees.

I rock back and forth, trying not to whimper too loudly.

Swift and silent.

We were meant to be safe here. Mama promised me.

A woman screams in the distance, and I shudder.

Thundering growls, smashing glass, and scrambling footfalls hit the floorboards. I inhale my cries and wrap myself around my bent knees.

Shadow Monsters are in the house.

I can't breathe… They'll rip me apart.

There's a scraping sound, like something is being dragged across the floor. Then it falls deadly silent.

All I hear are my breaths, the hammering of my heart.

Shadows pass over the wood slats just outside my door. With it comes a rancid meat smell. My stomach tightens so much, I think I'm going to vomit.

I flinch as another scream pierces the air, and I bite down hard on my bottom lip to stop myself from sobbing.

Someone slams into the wall just outside my hiding place. I shove backward, my spine pressing against the wall. Every inch of me is trembling ferociously, but I don't speak. Not a sound. Or they'll hear me.

A slurping sound mangled with screams fills my ears.

I want to yell, to run. My hands plaster to my ears and I tuck my chin into my chest, rocking back and forth.

Swift and silent.
Swift and silent.
Swift and silent.
Swift and silent.

I don't know how much time passes. Tears drench my cheeks. I can't stop trembling. I finally push forward and press my ear to the door. Sweat trickles down my back. My legs are cramping from sitting so long in one spot. *Mama, where are you?*

When I get too anxious to wait anymore, I unlatch the lock. The door creaks as I push it open. My heart stops.

I freeze on the spot.

Inhale.

Exhale.

Sitting here makes me an easy target. *Swift and silent.* So I force myself to look out.

The walls look like someone splashed red paint across them, but the sickening odor tells me it's blood.

Jaine lies on her back, her legs and arms twisted and broken. Her stomach lays splayed open. Shattered ribs poke up through the fabric of her pajamas. I'm going to be sick.

Terror bubbles on my throat.

"Don't be afraid of death," Mama would say. *"Our bodies are just vessels before we ascend to heaven. If you see someone dead, just look away and keep going."*

I whip my gaze away from Jaine and scramble out of the closet.

The silence is suffocating.

Moving fast through the old house barren of furnishings, I find no one around. I rush barefoot from one room to the next. Abandoned. *Mama, where are you?* Cold sweat sticks the fabric of my pajamas to my skin.

There are other homes in this homestead she may be hiding in, so I creep outside into the yard.

Rain falls as the bruised sky rumbles with thunder. A flash of lightning plunges across the heavens.

But I gasp at the sight before me.

Bodies lie everywhere, chaos all around me. Mothers. Children. Guards. A splitting ache tears through me. I should have tried to help rather than hide. I scan familiar faces, my stomach churning from the sickness, from seeing friends and neighbors torn apart and bleeding.

I hurry from one body to the next, searching for her face. Hope flickers inside me that she made it out alive. That she found a hiding space. I pivot around, and my gaze lands on a familiar face.

"Mama!" A cry bursts from my lips, and I rush forward, dropping to my knees by her side. Blood is pouring from the deep gash across her torn throat. I can't look at the injury, so I cup her face and place mine close to hers like she'd always do to me. Our noses touch; her skin is cool against mine. Tears fall and drip onto her cheeks. Dark brown hair spreads out around her head, her skin pale, tainted with blood. Everyone always says I'm beautiful like her with sharp cheekbones, small nose with a sprinkled with freckles, and a round face. But the only similarity I see right now are the light bronze eyes I look into.

"Mama," the word escapes my lips.

My insides shatter like glass.

"Mama! *Please*. Wake up." I hold her face, my arms trembling. "Please don't leave me." I won't survive on my own. I'm completely alone.

She never responds, and I just cry at her side. Mama is all I have left in the world. My breaths billow, and I hug myself. A cold wind cuts through my hair. The rain comes down heavily now, drenching me, but I don't move.

Mama will never drag me into her arms ever again or cover my face in kisses. She'll never wake me up with tickles. Or hold me tight at night when the storms come. I feel so lost. So angry. So scared. My breaths don't come easy as my heartbroken sobs float on the air.

Mama looks so peaceful lying down, her muscles relaxed as opposed to her always being tense when she was alive. My heart gives a painful throb when a gravelly snarl grows behind me.

I jerk my head up and twist around fast. Terror reverberates through my head.

A Shadow Monster stands at the corner of the house. Lanky and thin, his torn clothes hang loosely from his bony frame. He has no lips; they've been eaten away. Only teeth, broken and stained. That's all I see at first. Then the bulging eyes from the gaunt face. He is so skinny... starved.

I scramble backward up on my feet, panic kicking me in the gut.

He lurches forward, groaning.

Retreating, I want the world to open up and swallow me.

But the creature doesn't come to me. He falls to his knees in front of a dead woman and shoves his mouth into her torn stomach, eating. That slurpy sound makes me gag.

Bile hits the back of my throat. I recoil when someone brushes against my shoulder.

Spinning, I shriek to find another undead creature inches from me. Instinct kicks in, and I back away. Hair like straw dangles over her lifeless face. My heel hits something, and I fall. Hitting the ground, I shuffle backward, noting the fleshy, gory, torn-off leg I tripped over.

Fear pummels through me as my brain numbs. I can't do this. I can't.

The creature pounces.

I yell and flinch backward.

But it dives for the dead child beside me. My heart pounds in my throat.

The Shadow Monsters didn't see me. How? It's as though I'm invisible or something.

That's who I am. Invisible. I have to believe that or I won't move.

I scramble to my feet and find someone's disembodied finger stuck on my pajama pants with so much red gung.

Nausea pulses through me.

The undead's head snaps up in my direction, eyes falling to the stain. I shove the pants down my legs and toss them aside. I recoil as the creature eyes the pajamas crumpled on the ground.

Another creature who staggers on his feet bumps into me before pushing past me. A strangled cry escapes from my lips, and I slap a hand over my mouth to silence my sobs. I back away from the river of undead coming this way through the broken fence.

God, there are so many.

Shadow Monsters were once shifters just like me. Or maybe mere humans, or one of a number of other supernaturals in the world. Mama said the virus that destroyed our world didn't discriminate and took everyone it could, turning them into the undead.

Not one of the Shadow Monsters so much as looks my way, but they dart to the recently dead to feed. It's all they know.

My heart is beating too hard, too fast.

I don't know what's going on, but I have to get out of here before my strange luck runs out and they start noticing me. So I push past the horde of creatures.

Once clear, I run toward the main street, my feet now bare and bloody and in pain as I pound the worn path.

Jaine was right. *Swift and silent.*

CHAPTER 1

MEIRA

Five Years Later.
When it rains, it pours.

I used to fucking hate that saying, loathed it with a passion. Mostly because I didn't understand how true it really was. How when life delivers one sucker punch, it quickly follows up with several more just to make sure you aren't getting up.

I'm not an optimist. I accept that. Living in a world ravaged by a virus broke my spirit when I lost everyone I've ever known... including Mama.

"Move," barks a muscular, white-haired Alpha as he snatches my arm, squeezing the hell out of it. He drags me down the middle of a small aircraft that reminds me of a steel coffin with wings.

The ropes binding my wrists at my back are too tight. The friction rubs against my skin and it stings. I want to say something, but I'm still tasting the blood in my mouth from his backhand at my last demand to release me. So I say nothing and stumble alongside him to keep up.

There are no seats in this small aircraft, just small, round windows and women sitting on the floor on either side of me. Eight women, not including me. They sit with their backs to the walls, their hands cuffed to a single chain linking them all and anchoring them in place.

They each stare at me with fear in their gazes. Their clothes are torn and filthy. Bruises and cuts litter their arms and legs... God, they are all about my age, nineteen-twenty years old. Some are stunning, other ordinary, but they are all terrified.

Just like me, they were found in the woods at the wrong place, wrong time by the Ash Wolves. It's my fault for entering the Shadowlands Sector... their territory. I should have known better, but starvation messes with your head. I've been living alone for the past five years, scavenging what I can, avoiding the monsters in the woods and wolf packs alike.

Female wolf shifters are commodities, and apparently, only good for two things.

Mating with the intent to breed.

Or trading, which eventually leads to point one.

And lucky me, I'm being traded to another wolf pack in the far west of Eastern Europe. Just delaying the horrible inevitable mating coming my way. I will fight to the end before I ever give in to any Alpha.

I grit my teeth, not caring whom they send me to. I'll escape and run. That's all I've known since the undead monsters stormed into my home and killed everyone I knew. My gut aches at the memory, and my wolf whimpers deep in my chest, but I drive the thoughts away. Not now. I refuse to drown in the grief I can't shake.

The white-haired shifter pivots me around, then shoves me away until I hit the wall.

"Sit!" he growls, darkness gathering under his ice-blue eyes. He's a wolf Alpha; I smell it on him like the electricity in the air after a storm. The scent of wolf lingers on him too, and my own beast responds, acknowledging him. But the rumble in my chest is a warning for him to stay away. His presence leaves a bad taste in my mouth.

I slide down to my knees and sit on my heels.

"Caspian, are we ready to go? Just brought in the last one from Mihai's delivery," the man who brought me into the plane suddenly calls out, his attention cutting to the open door leading to the cockpit.

"Mad, get your fucking ass in here."

I tuck these shifters' names into my mind for later because knowledge is everything in a world that has fallen apart. Information can be sold to the right buyer or to extract oneself out of a sticky situation.

Mad huffs and drags a hand down his rugged face. He's not an ugly man... quite the contrary. He looks to be in his mid- to late twenties with strong angular lines on his face and a square jawline, broad shoulders, and a body made of muscle. Except my skin crawls. There's an aura about him that doesn't sit right. Then again, most males I've encountered have a similar effect on me. They want one thing from me. While all I want is to drive my knee into their groins.

"Fuck, man," the other man in the cockpit snarls the words.

"I swear to hell, Caspian. We're already running

late after Mihai insisted he got lost on the way here with the cargo. You better not fuck this up too." Mad's upper lip curls into a sneer as he marches forward and vanishes into the cockpit. From my angle, I watch him bend over to help the pilot, but I don't waste another second.

The fool has forgotten to link me up to the chain with the other women. A smug, satisfied smile spreads on my lips. Slowly, I lift myself to my feet, glancing the way we came, the main door still gaping open.

I glance over to the other women, their hands tied to a joint chain. I'll never release them without being caught first.

"Go," whispers the thin redhead next to me, her eyes flicking to the door and back at me.

An alarm screeches in my head that my chance to escape is narrowing the longer I wait.

My breath hitches, and I mouth, "*Sorry.*" I swirl around, my hands still tied behind me, and run as quietly as possible to the exit. Shivers ripple up my arms at the thought that I'll be caught.

I look behind me once more to find Mad still hasn't returned. Outside, the truck that drove us here is gone. I leap down onto the gravelly ground, my knees wobbling, but I manage to not fall over with my wrists restrained. Yay for me. Then I dart down the landing strip behind the aircraft. *Swift and silent.* I don't dare stop, and hope the pilot doesn't see me.

Running full tilt with my hands tied is harder than I expected, my shoulders swinging wildly back and forth in a see-saw manner.

Around me, pines stand tall and silent, the only witnesses to the direction I take. My pulse thumps in my ears. A quick look behind, and I'm far enough from the airplane to now slip into the dense woods and vanish from sight.

I don't know how long I've run, but I don't stop. The hill I'm scaling leaves my thighs burning. Ignoring the ache, I push forward.

The mistake is mine for going anywhere near a wolf pack in the first place. I've met enough females on my travels who have helped me out and told me whom to steer clear of.

Ash Wolves are at the top of this list in Romania. Their Alpha, Dušan, is a controlling shifter who rules the biggest pack in the surrounding countries, and he gained that position for a reason. He takes what he wants without mercy.

Other smaller packs exist here and there in Transylvania, along with rogue wolves. Most small towns that once existed in the mountains have been overrun by the undead. Fewer safe zones exist now for free women.

I grew up terrified of these woods made of teeth and claws. Except now, it's my home. The Shadow Monsters leave me alone for a reason I don't understand, and I accept the universe's fate. Now, I just need to navigate around the wolves who also call this land home.

At the crest of the hill, I stop to catch my breath and stare out over the ocean of pines as far as the eye can see. Across the horizon, a small craft ascends. Mad and Caspian taking those women to their new home, stolen from freedom. Guilt flares that I couldn't do more for them. Except as I watch them fly away, I know I made the right decision. I made the only possible decision.

Dušan

. . .

"Well, only eight arrived on the transport," Ander Cain states through the comm unit, the flare of anger narrowing his eyes. His golden irises glint on the screen with frustration.

I'm seething, but I don't show it to the X-Clan Alpha of Andorra Sector. We are business partners, and it took me a goddamn long time to build this relationship, to gain his trust. Until I get to the bottom of this, I'll keep my cards close to my chest. I am the Alpha of Shadowlands Sector and I don't back down, but I also won't jump into a fight unprepared.

"Your Second is here to confirm," Ander continues before turning the screen on his end to face Mad.

My Second stares at me with a stoic expression and rattles off his explanation. "Meira wasn't part of the transport."

Anger flares over my chest, and I clench my fists by my side. He'd given me a list of all the female wolves we captured last week, all nine of them destined for the X-Clan Wolves.

"How is that possible?" I roar, then I school my reaction in front of Ander.

"You'll need to check with Mihai. He was the last one seen with the cargo before we took off," he retorts, and he's pissing me off, passing the blame off to someone else. My pulse rages through my veins to remind him of his place.

"I thought I charged *you* with that task, Stefan?" I rarely use his given name, but he's testing my patience. As my Second, I have to trust him, and he needs to be fucking on top of everything we do.

Mad explains he was busy with Caspian in the cockpit, which only has me grinding my jaw. I can almost see the cogs turning, which tells me he's hiding something. He speaks with confidence, smooth and believable. But today, something's off.

"I expected you to manage the shipment," I hissed. "Which clearly did not happen. Put Cain back on," I snap, sick of seeing his face.

Ander reappears on the screen. Running my hand through my short, dark hair, I have no choice but to return the cargo he sent me as payment for the girls. While the X-Clan pack have power, technology, and advanced medicine to trade, what they lack are Omegas. Their Alphas can only mate and impregnate Omegas. And that is one thing I have in my territory. Female wolves, with a good number of them being Omegas. Their scent gives them away. So our exchange benefits both our packs.

The X-Clan and Ash Wolves are both shifters, but genetically, we're different. The X-Clan are immune to the undead.

While Ash Wolves aren't immune and we need to find fated mates for our wolves to connect through marking and sex. But with all the shit going on and a growing pack to protect from the zombies trying to break into our home, I don't have time for that kind of involvement.

To maintain our relationship with Ander, I reluctantly say, "You can hold back one of my cargos while I locate our missing Omega." This isn't what I want.

Ander studies me cautiously. Thick, black hair sits cropped short to his ears without a strand out of place. I visited his compound for negotiations. They still live in penthouses in high security buildings, while we made our homes among old ruins and wilderness.

We are wolves, one with nature, and the wild is where we belong. I wouldn't exchange that for anything.

After more back and forth with Ander on how we'll do this, considering he's already sent the shipment—adding complications to the situation—Mad interrupts, stepping into view on the comm screen. "I have a suggestion."

"And that suggestion is?"

"Caspian and I will stay here as collateral while you find the girl. Once found, Cain can send his own pilot to retrieve her, and then we'll make our way back to you afterward."

I don't miss the tightness around Ander's eyes at Mad's offer. Such a suggestion would leave me uncomfortable too, considering Mad just invited himself to stay in the Andorra Sector. What doesn't sit well with me is Mad not consulting with me first. I won't forget this when he returns home, along with the chaos he just caused with the missing girl.

Ander drags a thumb over his bottom lip, the decision weighing heavily on him.

Having little choice, I lift my chin and answer, "I accept those terms, if you're agreeable."

"You have a week," Ander responds. "We'll renegotiate at that point should the girl not be in your custody by that time."

Squaring my shoulders, I grin because I have no plans on letting this go on any longer than it already has. "Oh, I'll catch her by then. I'll be in touch soon."

I end the communication with a click of a button on the small screen on my office desk.

"Fuck! I'm going to murder Stefan."

My Third, Lucien, an Alpha also, stands in the doorway like a sentinel. Legs spread, arms folded over his broad chest. His recently cut hair draws attention to the scar across his collarbone from when we fought an attacking pack on our territory a few years ago. I placed him in charge of my warriors to lead my battles. He swore his loyalty to me after I saved him from a horde of undead when he was ten, and ever since, he's been by my side. I trust him.

"Do you think Mihai lost a girl?" Lucien asks.

"I doubt it. He's completed dozens of cargo deliveries. So what was special about this one?" I want to believe he didn't have another agenda.

"What about Mad?"

I exhale a heavy breath. "Something's not right with this delivery. I can feel it." Mad's always pushing the boundaries... Being my stepbrother, he thinks he can, except whatever game he's playing at ends the moment he returns home.

Up on my feet, I move to stand by my window overlooking the grounds below.

We live in an ancient medieval fortress, the land barricaded with lofty stone walls to keep the zombies out and protect my pack. I glance out to the wooden shacks layering the land inside the castle walls. I welcome any wolf shifters in danger into my protection under one condition: They submit to me as their Alpha. In exchange, they gain food and shelter.

With that comes the need for resources. And this is why my partnership with Ander is crucial. He provides technology, vehicles, weapons, and much-needed medicine that we can't otherwise acquire. It's this trade that gives me the chance to protect those in my pack and gain an advantage over other warring packs wishing to claim my territory.

My father was an Alpha, and he ruled with an iron fist. He gained followers through fear. But in the end, those men betrayed him.

Lifting my hand to my neck instinctively, my fingers run over the scar starting at my collarbone and going all the way up to the back of my ear. A little something from Father when I was eight for disobeying his order. He slashed me with a serrated blade as punishment.

"This is why you'll never make Alpha. You had the chance to kill me and never took it."

I ball my hands into fists, then turn to my Third.

"Get a group of Alphas together to hunt down that Omega and fix this fucking mess."

CHAPTER 2

MEIRA

Three Days Later.

My pulse races. Something is following me.

I twist around in the middle of the forest as a blur races amidst the dense woods toward me. Two legs, so definitely not an animal. A Shadow Monster? God, please don't let today be the day my good luck runs out.

I turn and run. The late-day sky cloaks the woods with an ominous gloom. I should have found a place to hide by now. Never stay out at night. All kinds of creatures slink out with the darkness.

My breaths are harsh and jagged.

A quick look over my shoulder shows a man is

thundering toward me like a beast. Nostrils flaring, his mouth gaping, and those huge eyes are locking on me. A glint of wolf sparks in his gaze.

My stomach drops.

Shit, not again. Please not again. I've kept away from the packs, and I haven't seen any shifters for days since escaping from the plane. Where the fuck did this one come from?

He pounces, slamming into me. I tumble to the ground with a grunt while I convulse with terror.

Strong hands snatch one of my ankles to haul me backward. I jerk around and kick him in the face. Then I scramble away from under him and bolt, my feet pounding to the ground. Panic knots in my gut. Sex is all he wants from me, and I shiver uncontrollably at the thought.

He throws himself on top of me, shoving me down. With a snarl, he rolls me over onto my back. The fuckhead clutches my throat and squeezes hard. Hot, rancid breath streams from his gaping mouth.

I punch his head over and over.

His lips curl upward, revealing razor-sharp canines, and he attacks. Teeth scrape and dig into the curve between my neck and shoulder. My flesh tears, the pain excruciating.

I scream and buck my body against him. He's so heavy and unmovable. Panic twists my mind.

Suddenly, he's ripped off me. I scramble to get up and reach the bite mark. It stings horribly, and I cup the wound to stop the bleeding that's worming through my fingers.

A cacophony of snarls and growls explodes in front of me. I recoil until I hit a tree. Fright paralyzes me as I clutch my wound.

Midnight-black fur is all I see from the wolf that rips into the other shifter. It's enormous, twice the size of a normal wolf, and in complete control of this battle. He leaps after the man, crashing down onto him and biting down onto his neck. The crunch of bone echoes, and I shudder.

Repulsed, I jump to my feet and charge out of there, the attacking man getting what he deserves.

A low rumble comes from behind me, and I spin around to find the black wolf trotting practically right on my heels. Trees crowd in around me, and I can't breathe. I'm suffocating with dread.

He growls at me, his nose creased, his fangs exposed. His fur bristles.

I cringe and almost die on the inside. I throw my hands out in front of me. "Please. I'm leaving your woods. Don't hurt me."

My heel catches on a tree root, and I'm falling. I scream as my heart slams to the back of my throat.

I hit the ground hard, and my hand instinctively seizes a thick branch near me. This isn't how I want to die. I hurl the stick at the wolf, who seems to be shimmering. His body convulses, fur shrinking, the long nose drawing into the body. Bones crack, the popping noise of skin splitting and knitting together. I've watched others transform, but I've never experienced it myself to know if it feels as painful as it looks.

Power pricks over my arms. The hairs on my neck shift.

It all happens in a heartbeat. Gone is the wolf, and in its place is a man standing over me completely naked. His icy blue eyes burn into me with the intensity of a raging storm.

My mind freezes over. I've avoided capture by wolves for the past few days by returning to the woods I'd been living in for years, so it's just my luck that I run into two wolves today. Fear twists my insides because I only barely escaped the others.

Shaggy, dark hair feathers around his chiseled face, cascading over his shoulders. He is huge, tall, and broad. Not that I expect anything else from an

Alpha. His scent smothers my senses, and my wolf pushes and prods against my insides to get a closer smell.

He studies me, his attention falling to my mouth, then lower. My skin pricks with a shiver, my nipples pebbled in response.

His chest ripples with muscles. A faint sprinkle of hair covers his pecs and sweeps down his stomach into a tight V, all the way down. He's all there, out and proud. A black thatch of hair, a flaccid cock. Even soft, he is *huge*. Heat pulses through me, and my insides clench.

I shove to my feet, not wanting this wolf's groin in my face. No matter how much my body warms at the sight. No matter how much I feel the throb of arousal between my thighs. What I need is to get out of here because the way he stares at me tells me he wants to touch me, to impregnate me.

"Look at me," he demands in a deep, smooth voice as he reaches out toward me, his fingers brushing softly along my shoulder near the wound.

I flinch away and cry out with pain, even as goosebumps travel over my arm where he's just touched me. I've been running all my life for survival. Attention from an Alpha isn't what I want. Power flares from him in waves. It prickles over my skin and weakens my knees, as if my wolf senses his authority. She whimpers inside me with a desperation to obey him.

Total betrayal. My own wolf… She lingers inside me, responding to this Alpha, but still hasn't made a show of fangs or fur when I call her forward.

He sniffs the air, his brow pinching, before he glances over to the wolf he attacked to save me. Except wolves don't aid anyone without wanting something in return.

"He bit you to mark you into a forced mating," he states, as if it isn't obvious.

"You don't say? It clearly didn't work," I answer, still clutching my bleeding injury. "I don't need your help."

"What is your name, girl?" He steps closer, and my eyes don't know where they want to look. They move up and down his body of their own accord.

My mind is reeling, trying to come up with an excuse. Anything to get me out of his tangled chaos. But my heart is banging too hard, and I hitch my next breath all the way to my lungs.

"It's Meira, right?" He smirks, noticing my inability to even control my own body.

"I have no name," I say, cringing on the inside. *Oh, shit, shit, shit.* He's related to Mad and Mihai. The wolves who kidnapped me and shoved me onto the plane.

His laughter irks me... what irritates me worse is that I like the way he sounds, how he tilts his head upward to laugh at me. How I desperately need him to put on clothes so I can gain control of my gaze once again.

"Well, you've saved me, and I'm thankful. Have a nice day." I turn and quickly lunge into a run. Every male wolf craves the same thing. A female to mate, to keep prisoner, to impregnate. The thought alone infuriates me, and I pump my legs faster.

His hand snatches mine and he whips me back around. My feet stumble, and I jerk to face him, crashing right into his bare chest. So much flesh everywhere. He's burning up and so hot to the touch.

I shove my hands against him and reel back, then swing a fist at him.

He moves unimaginably fast and catches my balled hand in his, stopping it short from clipping his face.

He grabs me by the scruff of my neck and wrenches me closer. "You're not dealing with a Beta. Remember that, because next time, I won't take well to almost being punched in the face."

Only an Alpha would be so arrogant. "Let me go!" I shout at him. I get the impression he could easily pick me up and swing me over his shoulder. I'm not blind to the way he studies me, dragging his gaze up and down my body.

My fists clench, and I spit at him, managing to hit him square in the chest. He glares at me, and he grabs my arm and then hauls me with him as he pushes into a march. "You're going to get yourself in a lot of trouble."

I fight him, stumbling behind him. "I'm not yours to abduct and keep."

"Who said anything about me keeping you? I have an Alpha who might be very interested in you."

Edgy anger fills me. He's going to send me off again to god-knows-what-monster in another country. I strain against his iron grip, and though I know it's futile, I never stop fighting.

"This would go a lot easier if you learned obedience. It can be quite rewarding." He arches a thick eyebrow with amusement.

That time, it's me who bursts out laughing, all fake and for show. "Does that actually work on anyone?"

There's a pause as he cups the side of my face harshly, holding me in place.

He sniffs me, inhaling my scent. All wolves carry a distinctive smell that easily identifies them but also reveals their status.

"You smell like Omega," he declares with accusation, his nose scrunching as if I'm not worth his time.

I cringe and bite down on my cheek to stop from blurting out that I don't belong to his hierarchy. That I'm not the lowest rank in the pack, where everyone will feel like they can take advantage of me.

Alphas rule, one taking leadership and controlling a pack of other Alphas, Betas, and Omegas. The handful of Alphas in a pack usually don't stray from the top, and are ranked in order of his Second, Third, and so forth. Betas are the fighters, both male and female, the work dogs of packs. The Omegas, on the other hand, are the ones who have no power and do as they're told their whole lives. Majority of females are Omegas or Betas. It's why Mama and I always found settlements without men. She taught me to stay independent, to be in control of my own life.

"You will learn your place. Or I can personally show it to you."

"You're an Ash Wolf, aren't you? Of course you are." My voice is shaky, and I hate that my reaction is so obvious.

He cuts me a dangerous look, and all I can do is stare into those pale blue eyes, the darkness of his long lashes, at just how perfectly handsome this beautiful man is. He has a strong jaw, a perfect nose, and full lips that leave me frightened by the way he makes me feel. I hate that I think he's anything but a brutal barbarian.

"And if I am?" he asks casually.

"I've heard things about your Alpha, and I don't want to be anywhere near that jerk." My temper flares at the thought that an Alpha like Dušan thinks he has a right to control everyone's life.

This man's gaze pierces into me, and I feel completely vulnerable under his scrutiny. "Really? What sort of things?" he probes, as if he's never heard the stories.

But I'll amuse him.

"That he's worse than the Shadow Monsters. That he kills all females after mating with them, terrified his child will eventually kill him to claim the position of Alpha. That he's ruthless."

"Those are severe rumors," he murmurs.

"Who said they were rumors?" I snap back at him.

His hand squeezes around my wrist, and I startle.

"So you've met the Alpha of Ash Wolves firsthand, then?" he asks.

"Well, no. Otherwise, I'd be dead. But I've spoken to enough people who tell a similar tale. Haven't you heard the saying, where there's smoke, there's fire?"

There he goes again, laughing, and I narrow my eyes at him.

I straighten my shoulders, trying another tactic since fists and screaming don't work. "*Please*. Can you find it in your heart to release me?"

"I suggest you come and find out the truth for yourself."

My stomach plunges to my feet, and the reality of him taking me to meet Dušan, Alpha of Ash Wolves, freezes my insides. The danger is real, my fate—sealed.

He hauls me deeper into the forest with long

strides. My knees are shaking as I wrack my mind to find an escape.

"You're a monster," I snarl, digging my heels into the dirt as he drags me. "And when your Alpha kills me and I'm six feet under, I hope the guilt chews you up for eternity."

"That's a long time to feel remorseful. I'm sure I'll get over it quickly." He smirks my way, like my survival is a joke.

I look at him with a painful fury that he doesn't seem to notice. He just rushes me through the woods. Me, the victim. And him, the warrior dragging me to my death.

CHAPTER 3

ALPHA

Fuck!

She's not what I expected. Gorgeous. Feisty. Tempting.

Her scent is like ambrosia, and it does something to me. Every inch of her calls to my wolf like no one has ever done before. My heartbeat races.

She's a wolf, yet the smell of humanity clings to her, along with something else. My nose pricks with the current of electricity beneath the smell, something almost sickly sweet. Every wolf carries a distinct scent that easily identifies their power, their status. We are born this way, nature dictating our future before our first breath into this world. But this girl… She doesn't carry the rippling power of an Alpha or Beta. Omega? Yes, but she smells differently.

She has no clue what she is either. I can see it in her lost, wild gaze. I feel it in her presence. Living day to day out in the woods. Like most of the female wolves we pick up, she's just trying to survive. On her own, she won't last out here. If the undead don't get her, the rogue wolves who lust over females to rut will sniff her down.

I'm doing her a favor by taking her. Though she doesn't think so, considering the way she fights me, digging her heels into the ground to slow us down. I'm seconds from tossing her over my shoulder and slapping that tight ass until she conforms.

The Omegas we catch become obedient almost immediately in the presence of an Alpha, their wolves taking control of them.

But not this hellcat. A growl rumbles in my chest, and I curl my fists.

There is something very different about this girl, and I intend to find out what.

Her obstinate behavior confirms she's grown up as a wildling in the woods and most likely hasn't been around too many males. I've searched the surrounding woods for the past couple of days and found no females. I only found her, once I extended the radius of my search. She has to be Meira. She fits the description perfectly, down to the beauty spot at the corner of her left eye.

"How far is your lair?" she asks sharply as she glances at the forest swaying in the breeze, the shadows dancing amid the trunks.

What is she searching for? The undead? Those bastards come out of nowhere. Where there's one, there are plenty. They travel like a swarm, so on the bright side, the numerous feet trampling the ground make them easily heard when they approach. My ears prick for any sounds in the distance… Nothing yet. The ones who survive the plague learn to assimilate and be quick on their feet.

Get bitten, and you become infected in a few hours. For that reason, we need to hurry. We have to get to my car down the hill before sunset. Otherwise, the other creatures that make the shadows their home will emerge. They don't make sounds; they attack without notice. Beasts who hunt only at night for fresh meat.

"If you'd stop fighting me," I point out, "we'd arrive sooner."

She watches my mouth as I speak but then tears

her gaze away angrily. She's clutching her neck, blood trickling through her fingers, but it doesn't keep her from glaring at me with fury.

"I'm not afraid to remain in the woods," she says with venom in her voice. "Maybe we should spend the night in the forest?"

I shake my head. "Nobody wants to stay in the forest at night. I'm not buying whatever game you're playing."

I've only just met her and already, she infuriates me. She's just a tiny thing, five-foot-two or -three, compared to me at six-foot-two. A curvy body, her breasts high and round. Hair the color of the surrounding trees' bark flutters halfway down her back. Shorter strands hang loose around her beautiful face. My fingers tingle as I imagine twisting her locks around my hand and gripping them as I fuck her from behind.

Fuck! I don't need those thoughts in my mind, not while I'm naked. And walking around with a raging hard-on is not fucking comfortable.

"I thought you would have liked games," she teases, antagonizing me. "It's what you Alphas do, right? Chase down females to make them your possessions?" She pierces me with the most beautiful pale bronze eyes. I've never seen that eye color before, but it's so much more than just a shade. They're shaped to look permanently sad, like she's experienced too much sorrow in her life. When she doesn't snarl at me, she almost looks like she might start crying. Flawless skin with a sprinkling of freckles over her nose, and my gaze falls to the rosy full lips. Who is this girl?

The dripping blood from her neck catches my attention, the rivulets rolling down her shoulder and into the material of her tee. How long before she draws the undead to us with the scent?

I pause and pivot in front of her. She flinches back, clearly scared of me. I'll admit that her reaction both excites and upsets me. I'm a twisted bastard that way.

"What are you doing?" She looks at me with narrowing eyes, as if unsure whether she ought to trust me or not.

She wears a blue skirt that falls to her knees, the fabric torn from the fight, and a black tee two sizes too small for her, revealing a line of creamy silk stomach.

Like her clothes, her sneakers are stained with mud and long overdue for a wash. I reach down and grab the hem of her skirt where I spot a rip in the fabric.

"Hey!" She reaches down to push my hands away, but I tear the chunk of long material from the base of her skirt so fast, she doesn't see it coming. I shove her shoulder to turn her away from me before tearing the rest of it from all around. With a final jerk, I rip the strip free.

She stumbles on her feet, her eyes bulging out of their sockets. The earlier dress now sits above mid-thigh, revealing gorgeous, toned legs.

She snarls. "What the hell did you do that for?"

I seize her by the arm and haul her closer. "Keep quiet." Quickly, I wrap the torn material over the bite mark and under the opposite arm, twice over. She fights me, but I hold her roughly. I'm not playing.

I need this done fast, yet awareness of how close we are ripples over my skin. Her scent sinks through me, making it almost impossible to concentrate. A heady mix of pheromones flares within me in response to her. My cock throbs. A primal hunger pulses inside me to protect this female from all other males, to claim her. Take her.

No female has ever affected me this powerfully before. I grind my back teeth and I jerk her forward, a bit harder than I meant to.

"You have no right to—"

"I have every right," I growl and swing away, drawing her with me by the arm. "If it means it will save our lives and stop you from collapsing from blood loss, I will do what it takes." My pulse is out of control, and a possessiveness over her swallows me. What the hell is going on with me?

Her heartbeat accelerates. I can feel it beneath my fingers as I grip her wrist while she snarls at me, baring perfectly white teeth. No chipped or broken teeth. She will be a good exchange for the other pack.

Except adrenaline laces my blood, my wolf surging forward at the thought, demanding we claim her.

When our gazes clash, I get a glimpse of her vulnerability. And damn, it draws me in even further.

My wolf slinks through me, insisting she belongs to us and we need to mark her now. Except something feels off. She feels different. And I won't jump to conclusions about finding my fated mate that quickly.

I always thought I'd know when I sensed my mate... but this girl isn't what she seems, so how can I trust what I feel? It almost seems as if she's hiding behind an invisible veil.

Once we get back home, I'll work out what's going on.

Her cheeks blush each time she glances my way, her eyes dipping down my body. Her embarrassment at my nudity doesn't fade, and she keeps looking away. I don't understand her reaction. She's a wolf… after transformations, we are nude. Natural as breathing and yet her face is red. She has no control of her roaming eyes.

Once we eventually reach a valley with a small running river, I pause, holding her closer with one arm around her narrow waist despite her grumbles. No sign of rogue wolves or undead nearby. The woods surrounding us are silent. I sniff the air to confirm we are alone. I didn't realize how far I'd traveled to find this hellcat. A group of five of us went in opposite directions in the woods to track her.

"Drink and let's wash your wound. We have a fair distance to travel."

I expect her to argue, but instead, she crouches and cups her hands under the clear, running water and draws it to her mouth to drink. Fresh water streams from her wet hands, falling back down to the surface of the river in large drops.

I do the same and fill my stomach.

She unravels the torn material I tied across her wound and pushes her long, umber brown hair over her shoulder. Then she cups more water and splashes it over the bite mark. It flows across her bare shoulder and soaks into her top. The fabric sticks to the perfect curves of her breasts.

My throat goes dry as I stare at the beads of water rippling over her collarbone and sliding beneath her top. A heavy desire closes in around me with the weight of a mountain.

The last streaks of sunlight glint against her raised face, and her bronze eyes seem to glow beneath the flare. Her gorgeous mouth parts as she exhales.

My groin clenches tight.

Such a beautiful creature. Whoever she is, I need to claim her.

I'm burning up to reach over and taste her, to mark her myself. The bite piercing her flesh bubbles with fresh blood. A fiery savagery rips through me at seeing the shifter's teeth blemishing her perfect skin. I crave to take her, to bury my face into her neck and taste her. To make her mine.

She runs her fingers over the injury and winces.

"How long have you been living in the woods

alone?" I ask, trying to understand more about her, and also to distract myself from the effect she has on me.

She stiffens and doesn't look at me. "A few years."

"Alone? You've done well to survive this long." A few years? Fuck, that would drive anyone crazy.

She nods as she wraps the fabric back over her bite mark. I reach over and help her tie a knot to keep it in place. As a wolf, she should heal quickly.

"I have my ways," she says. I see the hunger behind her eyes, the wolf inside her wanting to make a connection. But something doesn't feel right.

The snap of twigs reaches me.

I freeze, my gaze shooting across the narrow river to where the sound comes from. A shadow flitters amid the trees. My lungs seize.

A figure lurches forward... an undead... A lanky man wearing no shirt, his decaying chest covered in open scratches. He moans loud enough to alert others nearby to join him.

"Fucking great." We'll be swarmed in no time.

Meira spins out of my grasp and runs back the way we came.

My pulse is on fire, and I throw myself after

her. Seizing her arm, I drag her back into the woods fast. She fights me, as if facing an undead is a better option for her. I pray the blood in the water and near the bank distracts them enough that they won't follow us.

Fury churns in my gut.

"Let me go! They're after *you*."

I figure she's being her usual, complimentary self. "Where do you hide?" I demand.

But she says nothing, like suddenly the danger across the river isn't her problem. "If I shout right now, they'll be on us in no time." There's a challenge in her eyes, a threat. "Release me, and I'll tell you where you can go hide. Otherwise, you'll die tonight."

A sinister grin splits her mouth, and I have no doubt she means every word.

My wolf unleashes a low moan that bleeds up my throat.

I hear the splash of water, and my heart rages against my ribcage. A shudder rushes down my spine.

Squeezing her arm harder, I pull her close so we're face to face. "Listen. If I die in these woods, my entire pack will be scouring the woods to find you. Do you know what they do to Alpha killers?" I snarl.

She shrugs nonchalantly, and fuck, she is testing me. "They will hand you around to be taken by every single male." Of course I'm lying, but she doesn't know that. "Help me and I'll be sure you're taken care of."

She swallows loudly, the color draining from her cheeks. It takes her a while to think this through. "If the undead kill you, no one will think I'm to blame in any way."

I transfer my hand to her wrist and hold her. She thinks on her feet, and I like that about her.

The hatred she tosses at me makes me smirk. Then we're moving with haste through the woods.

She navigates the forest expertly, even with night closing in. She knows this location very well. We take a sharp left between two lofty pines into a denser part of the landscape. Pine needles litter the ground, and I note a small worn path. She's been living in this location for a while now.

We pause, and then she's reaching for a rope ladder dangling from an enormous tree. I glance up to find a platform overhead.

I didn't see *this* coming. She's built herself a treehouse to escape the dangers. Secretly, I'm in awe of her survival skills. How has she managed to go this long without an undead attack? She still had to hunt for food.

When the crunch of foliage comes from nearby, I grab the rope ladder and begin climbing. I glance up, only to see the perfect view of her ass in black underwear under her skirt. I shouldn't feel anything, but heat bursts through my veins until it feels like I'm on fire.

She scrambles up onto the platform, and I race up. I wouldn't be surprised if she cuts the cords and throws me down to the monsters.

CHAPTER 4

MEIRA

*N*ight spreads her wings over the forest.

Usually, I sit up here, feeling safe in my wooden home, a simple box I made of thick branches I bound with rope to build walls and a roof. The branches are uneven, leaving gaps in the walls that blink at me with darkness. Just like me, it has imperfections. But I love it here.

I cut a glare across to the wolf shifter next to me, who's going to tear all this away from me.

He sits with his knees bent and arms draped over them, staring at nothing in particular. It must be killing him to have to hide up here with me instead of dragging me back to his pack to appear a hero to his Alpha.

"How have you survived alone so long?" he asks.

Shadows dance across his gorgeous face, and he doesn't even look at me, instead dropping his gaze to the wooden floor between his bent legs. I don't answer, except I remember Mama would always say: *Knowledge is power*. And this shifter has information that might help me understand the wolf packs so I can better avoid them.

"Life can be savage," he continues.

My response comes flying out. "You're an Alpha, working closely with the big wolf himself, so I doubt your life is that difficult." I regret the snarkiness in my voice immediately. I remind myself all of us who are left behind are still alive because we faced hell itself to not perish.

When he doesn't respond and guilt gnaws on my insides, I say, "Sorry, shouldn't have said that." We may be enemies, but in truth, are we any different? We're both making a life amid a horrendous virus that wiped out so much of the population. We're survivors, no matter who we are on the inside.

"This isn't where I wanted to end up," I admit. "But the endless strain of surviving forces you to make do."

"I haven't met many who are happy with their situation. But shit happens."

"Shit like kidnapping females and selling them to other packs like cattle?"

He turns toward me, and there's fire behind his eyes. I've touched a sore point. "No females are ever harmed. They're kept safe and looked after. That is part of our agreement."

"But we're still taken against our will, aren't we?"

"Aren't we all trapped by the undead? Forced to live in small settlements, make the best with what we have? So what's the difference?" His voice darkens, his words clipped.

"The difference is that we should get a choice if we go to the other pack or not. How do you sleep at night?"

He barks a loud laugh. "Count yourself lucky the Ash Wolves rule over Romania because things would be a shit show for everyone if we didn't. There are hardly any humans left in this territory after the virus, and the wolves moved in to dominate. But that shifter who attacked you earlier wouldn't care if you had food or shelter. He'd tie you to a tree and just rut you until you perished. Those are the kind of monsters that are out there. So, yes, I sleep soundly knowing I am making a difference." The depth and sincerity in his voice touches me more than I expect. It doesn't settle the fire in my chest about getting kidnapped and shipped off, but there's something almost beautiful about his passion to make a difference. My earlier hate for him eases a bit.

A sudden ache lashes across the middle of my stomach. It hits me with a sharpness pulsing through my limbs. The sickness has never left me after so many years. That feeling overwhelms me, and I hug myself, leaning forward as the wave rushes over me. It comes and goes, but as of late, I've noticed it hits me more frequently, as though it's building inside me. I'm scared it's my wolf wanting to come out, this damn beast who has tortured me my whole life.

"Are you hurt?" he asks.

I shake my head. "It's just hunger pains."

He reaches forward and grabs one of my green apples from the bowl I have in the corner. "Eat this."

I accept the offering and look over to him. Beneath the tough exterior, he does give a fuck about others. I bite into my apple, its sweetness coating my tongue and the juices dribbling from the corner of my mouth.

He stares at my lips, at the way I wipe away the mess. His lips part as he watches me. Is he going to lean in and kiss me?

The thoughts steal my breath, beads of sweat pooling between my breasts. My body has never reacted this way before, with such arousal and need all rolled up into a bubble ready to burst inside me. And just from a single thought.

But he never leans in closer or kisses me. He sits there, staring outside and biding his time.

By the time I finish eating, the ache settles, and I toss the apple core outside through the narrow doorway. A cool breeze curls inside the treehouse, and with it comes the shifter's woodsy, wolf scent. My heart skips a beat, blood rushing through my veins. What is wrong with me?

I rub my arms, noticing the goosebumps covering his skin.

I turn to the small bundle of clothes I've stolen during my searches from homesteads I've ransacked. I pull out an oversized black coat. It was made for a large man, and I've been using it as a blanket.

"Take this. It will warm you."

"I'm fine," he responds, staring straight ahead. "Cover yourself."

"I can see you're cold," I admit, hoping that if I show him care and compassion, he'll do the same with me if the time comes. He's opened up to me, so it's the least I can do. "You know, it's okay to accept help."

When he looks over at me, all I can focus on are his pale blue eyes, how much he reminds me of a wolf. This man screams *predator*, and he embraces what he is. Unlike me. I don't know what I'm supposed to be. I'm not a complete wolf since I still haven't had my first transformation, and I'll never be complete. I'm broken and unwanted because of what lives inside me from the lack of transforming.

"Will *you* accept help if I offer it?" he asks, his brow arching upward.

"Depends on what your offer is. Help is subjective and means different things to everyone. I love this home I built. It gives me the freedom to come and go, to not be controlled by anyone. So I don't need aid."

"But you're alone. We all need someone, no matter how strong we think we are."

"You know what happens when you get close to

people? They end up dying, and it breaks you. So yeah, alone suits me perfectly fine." I drag the coat over my legs and up to my chin to keep the cold away.

"Better to have felt that pain. Then at least you knew love."

His harsh response sinks into me and resonates at my core. I had Mama, who adored me, but my father walked out on us when I was six after a huge argument with Mama. I remember the screams, the indents in our walls from his frustrated punches.

"I can't protect either of you!" he'd shout. *"Meira is weak because of me. She'll always be an outcast."*

Even after all these years, his words are a kick to the gut. My throat thickens at the memory that he was too weak, too weak to stay with us. He left because of me in the end. I bite down on my cheek until it hurts, just to stop the agony of the past.

We fall into another silence and I feel lost, unsure where I belong in this world. I know with certainty that being a slave isn't my destiny. I've been hiding for years behind the veneer of this forest, and it's exactly where I want to remain unnoticed. Here, I can do what I want and no one judges me.

My pulse races and now all I can think about is how I'll get away from this shifter. The moment I hear him sleeping, I'm out of here. Sure, it sucks that I will have to find a new forest to build my treehouse, but it'll be worth it to get away from the wolf pack. I don't need anyone.

"You should get some rest," he remarks. "We're leaving at first light."

Only I should get some sleep? So he has no plans of resting? He'll watch me. Gritting my teeth, I shuffle down and onto my side on the blanket I use for my bed. The small size of the treehouse doesn't permit me to sleep stretched out, so I curl in my legs and roll away from the shifter. I doubt he'll be able to stay up all night, so I'll bide my time.

He shuffles behind me, the wood groaning under his weight. Next thing I know, he's lying down behind me, laying with his chest against my back. Despite wearing no clothes, his skin is scorching hot against me, and the heat overwhelms me.

I stiffen, flexing my shoulders.

His hand loops around my waist as he drags me harshly against him.

I gasp and wriggle to escape, but he holds me in

place. "You're not running from me," he growls in my ear.

My heart stutters.

"I can't sleep like this," I insist.

"Get used to it."

I freeze for a moment, then turn my head over my shoulder to see the smirk on his face. "What do you mean?"

"Come on now, little hellcat. You're not that naive. What do you think an Alpha will want to do with a gorgeous Omega like you?"

I grit my teeth and writhe against him. "I'm not a possession."

He laughs behind me. Asshole loves seeing me angry. Swinging a leg over me, he uncovers me in the process and pushes closer. His cock presses against my ass with only the thin fabric of my skirt and underwear between us.

I go to move, but he keeps me locked in place. A twitch pokes my ass cheeks, then another twitch, and it doesn't take long for his cock to become hard. And hell, he feels so large.

"You clearly have no control," I say.

"If you keep wriggling, you'll have a real problem on your hands."

His words have me stilling, and he just laughs at me.

"I hate you," I blurt out.

"Good. I wouldn't expect anything less. Now shut your eyes."

Drawing them shut, I know sleep won't come. Crap, why does he have to smell so divine? All I can think about is how good it could feel to have him against me, skin to skin. I imagine his cock sliding in between my legs, and a pulse throbs at my core.

His breath hitches behind me.

I freeze.

Oh fuck, he can smell my heat.

Alpha

Her sugary scent teases my senses and fills my nostrils. Her heat burns through me... little vixen wants me just as I want her. My balls are drawn up and feel heavy. I'm really not doing myself any favors here. She's promised to someone else. But she'll escape during the night if I fall asleep, and being a light sleeper, I'll feel her moving out from under me. So I hold her close.

She keeps wriggling that tight ass of hers, and the more she pushes me, the more I won't be able to control what I do next. All I can picture is me driving into her, filling her, making her scream. I've never felt so desperately fucking horny before. What I feel is that instantaneous lust, and my body is alive, ready to claim her. I do my best to hold on to my sanity. I glance down to where her coat and skirt has ridden up over her rear. The thin fabric of her black underwear follows the curve of her ass. My dick pulses at the thought of touching her everywhere.

My heart and I lie there with her in my arms, drowning in that sweet vanilla and clementine fragrance, mixed with her slick heat.

Holding her tight, my fingers graze the soft skin of her stomach, my cock pressing against her ass cheeks.

She suddenly shuffles to roll over, her ass rubbing over my dick, sending me ridiculously close to the edge of losing my mind. I hiss an inhale as she twists to face me.

"That's better," she grumbles as she curls her

body to ensure no part of her touches my now painfully solid erection. She drags that coat over her and wraps herself up in it with just her head sticking out. Her mouth tugs into a grin with a look of satisfaction, like she's won. Hell, I haven't even started if that's the game she wants to play. But I won't let myself go there. Because if she begs me to take her, I won't stop until I have her beneath me and writhing.

Her breath sears across my bare chest, and she looks up at me with amusement. Her pale bronze eyes remind me of a sunset after a violent storm that shakes the earth. That's what meeting her feels like.

"Good night," I say, and with my hand still around her back, I wrench her toward me.

She gasps as her body slams up against mine, my dick nestled perfectly between us. With a grin curling my lips, I close my eyes.

I feel her hatred setting off sparks of awareness across my body.

"Why do you even care if I go back with you? You can tell your Alpha you didn't find me."

I crack open one eye to her glare, then another. "You want me to lie? I'm guessing you've never been in a pack environment before. You'll learn very soon."

"Heard enough to know the hierarchy." Those gorgeous eyes narrow, and I know exactly why she's so angry. But in a pack, she'll be safer than out here. The X-Clan has agreed to care for all females I send them.

"No free animal enjoys capture," I explain. "But once they accept their new life, they realize the benefits."

She gives me a dubious look. "Really? You just referred to me as an animal needing to be broken in. Bet *you're* popular with the females." She huffs and flashes her vicious glare my way.

"Putting it crudely, some wild wolf shifters need breaking in for the benefit of the whole pack to work in harmony. Everyone knows their roles, and together, we are stronger." But she won't be my problem for long. Her new Alpha can have fun taming this one.

"You keep telling yourself that."

I grit my teeth. One more remark and she'll be lying over my lap and receiving my palm over that little ass. I tighten my grip around her. I came out here for one simple mission. Find the missing girl and return her.

She begins to fidget with the collar of the coat

covering her, a nervous twitch, but soon after she settles down and closes her eyes.

Her heat continues to twist and curl through the air until I'm encased in it. I watch her face as her head rests on a folded hand. There is no denying her beauty—the dark hair spread out behind her, the perfect lines of her small cheekbones and nose, her full, luscious lips... the same lips that said everything she shouldn't have. Suddenly, her nostrils flare, as if sensing me looking at her.

I smile to myself.

Beneath the moon's hue, she looks intoxicating.

She is too perfect.

Too beautiful.

Way too distracting.

And not mine.

CHAPTER 5

MEIRA

My eyes flutter open, and I'm falling. Panic slams into my chest. I shudder, my arms jutting out to catch myself. Except my wrists are bound together with rope.

"Settle down," the Alpha growls in my ear, his arm looped around my waist as I realize I'm hanging over his shoulder while he climbs down from my treehouse.

He reaches the ground, and I slide down his body until my shoes touch soil. Our faces are so close, I can see the silvery flecks in his irises catching the sunlight. My heartbeat races in my chest.

I hate his quirk of a smile as my breasts drag down his chest. He may have the body of a god, all naked and insanely sexy, but I want nothing to do with him.

"Untie me," I hiss, jutting out my bound wrists to him. "I can't believe you tied me up while I slept."

In reply, he reaches over and grabs the rope dangling from my bonds, pulling me behind him. "Let's move."

"Are you fucking serious? A leash? I'm not a dog."

"You're my little wolf," he says with a small smile as he glances over his shoulder.

My feet stumble after him, and I'm seething on the inside. "Last night, I actually thought you might be an okay wolf. I even hated you less. But now, I loathe you more than the Shadow Monsters roaming these woods."

He looks at me, his lips pinched. "That's a lot of hatred."

I tug against him, but he doesn't give an inch, hauling me into faster steps. Last night, I should have shoved him out of my treehouse.

"Just behave and this will be over in no time," he suggests, like he's doing me a favor.

Fuck him. I fight him the whole way, making him drag me and work for every inch.

We've been walking for hours, ducking low branches, trampling prickly shrubs, and stepping over dead logs. He brought with us several apples I've already eaten, and still my stomach still growls for food.

He even permitted me to relieve myself behind a tree. While he held the rope, of course. The shame. I will make him pay.

Coupled with that, how can we not have come across any undead yet? The sun sits directly above us when we finally step out of the thick woods.

He looks left and right down an old worn road, as if something is meant to be waiting for him. Overgrown grass and weeds press in at the edges, swaying in the breeze.

"Did they forget about you?" I say in a mocking tone. "So much for the pack who cares. Seems you're just another shifter who doesn't matter to the vile Alpha who's abandoned you out here. Is he really worth risking your life for?"

He stares at me, and those blue eyes flicker with the faintest smear of something dark. Something dangerous.

The threatening look leaves me trembling. This shifter carries power.

"Keep quiet and move fast. Or I'll carry you the

whole way and you will not be conscious." The gravelly edge in his voice delivers his promise. He's worried about how vulnerable he is out here to the undead.

He swings left and tugs me behind him roughly.

I contemplate screaming and making a ruckus, but there are no guarantees the Shadow Monsters are even close enough to hear me. And I believe him when he says he will knock me out.

We walk onward, past lofty pines with the sun heavy on our backs. I suck in a harsh breath as a warm breeze swooshes through my hair. I swallow over my dried throat, and the muscles in my thighs ache from the steep downhill descent.

Twigs snap to my right, and I twist around to find a deer staring at us from the woods. The shifter guiding me doesn't even look at the animal, just sniffs the air.

"I may have no choice but to do as you say right now, but don't think that I am in any way obedient." I should have done more to let the Shadow Monsters take him yesterday. Slowed down. Fallen down. Something. But his words terrified me because the wolves would return. They'd catch my scent on him and never stop hunting me.

He looks over at me and considers my words. "If you follow my instructions, you will be safe. There's nothing for you to fear."

I want to laugh. I lift my bound wrists to prove my point. "And secondly, your Alpha is sending me to another pack, so don't lie to me."

"I can guarantee that you won't be harmed. I will never trade with brutes."

My heart pounds.

He talks as if he is someone who has influence over what happens to me once I reach the Ash Wolves pack. Except the stories I've heard of the Ash Wolves Alpha paints him as a barbarian. A different woman every night. He whips shifters who don't hunt for food. And any newborns in his pack are banished. Well, I struggle to believe that last rumor since that makes no sense to growing his pack. But the other stories sound real enough.

"Right, a lesser shifter can have such power over the Alpha of Ash Wolves." I tear my gaze from his.

But I feel him watching me from behind hooded eyes. "You need to know who I—" His words cut off, and I look around to see him staring down the road. A black vehicle is coming our way. The faint crunch of wheels on asphalt reaches me.

My stomach sinks right through me because now my capture feels real. With only this shifter, I feel I have the chance to escape, but once with the pack, I'll be watched. A shiver grips my spine.

The shifter draws me to the side of the road by an arm and holds me close.

"You don't have to do this," I say, my voice desperate. I'm about to be taken into the pack that rules this whole damn country. I won't be able to escape, and whatever freedom I thought I had will be a distant memory.

He waves at the approaching vehicle, ignoring me.

"Please! Set me free." I reach for his arm, touching him. "I don't want to be sold or be someone's slave. I'll die. Your Alpha doesn't even have to know you found me. I'll slip into the woods and you'll never see me again."

When he looks over at me, I search his eyes for sympathy…for anything to show me he isn't the monster I believe him to be.

"I can't do that, Meira." His words are sharp and clipped.

"I hate you."

The jerk just smiles as the black four-wheel drive vehicle grinds to a halt in front of us.

My legs wobble, and my mouth falls open to beg once more, but the driver pushes the car door open, stealing the words from my lips.

A man steps out of the car. Six-foot-three, slightly taller than the shifter next to me. His pale, steel-gray eyes scream wolf. He's broad-shouldered and rugged and smoldering. My heart is pounding wildly, my lungs gasping for air.

Despite his burly size, he stares at me with intense interest, like he knows something I don't. I'm surprised he's not burning hot in his long-sleeved, button-down shirt under this sun. Dark jeans hang low on his narrow hips, and he's wearing cowboy boots, which I find strange. He's got a head full of deep brown hair, a square jaw with strong lips, and a slight shadow covering his jawline, adding to the whole mountain man look. There is something extremely sexy about him, and mysterious… and that isn't what I ought to feel.

He stands tall and proud, his chin high, carrying himself with arrogance. Is he the Alpha of Ash Wolves?

Amid these two, I'm out of place, extremely short in my sneakers and completely breathless.

"Lucien, I was thinking you'd abandoned me,"

jokes my captor to the newcomer, and I suspect that little comment is a jab at my earlier remark.

I stare daggers at him.

Lucien does a double-tap of his fist to his chest before giving a slight bow of his head. "Dušan, I had no doubt you'd find your way back." He chuckles as if that's an inside joke between the two.

Wait!

What?

Did I hear right? My gaze flips between the two men and lands on Dušan.

The shifter whose arms I'd fallen asleep in. The man who had his erection poking my butt.

I can't breathe.

He was Dušan, the Alpha of Ash Wolves this whole time and he didn't tell me!

His expression is full of mirth, enjoying himself at seeing my shock.

Surprised? He may not say it, but I see it scribbled all over his face.

He let me say all that stuff about him, and he just listened to me. Heat crawls up my neck, but nothing compares to the anger burning in my chest.

Blinking at the men, I'm at a loss for words. I

have no idea why my wolf seemed interested in this Alpha and wanted me to sidle up closer to him. She must have her wires crossed because this Alpha is everything I don't want in a partner. Arrogant. Dominant. Pushy.

I rip my stare from his and find Lucien's eyes piercing through me. His attention drags up and down my body, taking all of me in. A nervous excitement builds inside me, which is wrong. Nothing about either of these shifters should have my body responding to theirs, but it does. I overheat, and my nipples harden against the fabric of my top. Beneath their gazes, I feel exposed, as though I'm the one standing in front of them naked.

Lucien's gaze swings up to my eyes, and I can't look away from those hypnotic steel-colored orbs crowned by long dark lashes. "Is this her? Meira?"

"Yeah," Dušan responds, shooting me a satisfied look. "She's feisty, so watch the claws."

I sneer at him as he hands over the rope tied around my wrists to Lucien, then strides over to the rear of the vehicle.

Words graze my mind, but from utter shock, they refuse to come out. I'm stuck with two shifters who have my wolf rumbling for closeness, yet who are kidnapping me from my freedom.

"Put her in the back and let's get out of here," Dušan orders as he opens the rear door of the vehicle. He pulls out clothes, then steps into the blue jeans with frayed hems. As he tucks himself away, he lifts his gaze toward me and winks.

I'm fuming.

Lucien snatches my elbow and drags me to the back door of the vehicle before he opens it for me. "After you."

I lift my tied hands to climb in and push myself up, finding it harder to do with my wrists bound.

There's a shove at my back, and I fall forward onto the seat. I turn my head. "You're a real charmer, you know that?"

The door smacks shut just as Dušan closes the rear one.

"Assholes!" I yell as both men stand outside, whispering in private. I search the floor and back of the car for any weapons. Only clothes in the back. I shuffle across to the opposite door and tug at the handle. Locked. Of course it is.

The pair outside walk back to the car and jump into the front seats.

My stomach lurches as we take off down the road.

Dušan leans back and looks at me from the front. Blue eyes stare at me, burning like an inferno through me as he fixes his gaze on my face. "Get comfortable. It's a long drive."

I look away from him and stare out the window as we pass the forest. The place I once called home. Driving past it feels bittersweet. There is no way out of this for me.

CHAPTER 6

MEIRA

A shiver passes over me as we turn and drive up a long, narrow road. We've been going for hours up through the rocky hilltop of the Carpathian Mountains, and the closer we get to Dušan's pack, the more my stomach feels uneasy.

Outside, undead linger near and more stumble out of the woods. This is never a good sign, because it means they've sensed blood or they remember feeding in this location before. They remember areas.

We drive up to a pair of solid metal gates standing at least fifteen feet tall. A similar fence with barbed wire across the top stretches out on either side of the gate and around the whole settlement. The place looks ominous with a penitentiary vibe.

Gigantic pines lean low over our path, but the ones near the settlement have been chopped, with only stumps remaining. They've done everything possible to stop the undead and intruders from getting into their settlement.

I look ahead and spy an enormous medieval building beyond the fence and up on the hill. My mouth falls open with utter surprise.

"Your pack lives in a damn castle?" I gasp, staring at the steadfast stone walls, the pointy towers, the crenellations across the top. I've read about such places in books that Mama found for me when we'd ransack abandoned homes. But this is first time I've been near one.

"It's Râşnov Fortress," Dušan explains. "Knights built this place long ago to protect local villages against invasion from other countries. The Saxons later expanded the structure. And now, the Ash Wolves call this place home."

I nod, unable to stop staring up at the fortress that seems to take up most of the mountain. This whole time, I assumed the wolves lived in wooden shacks in the forest to keep safe from the Shadow

Monsters in the most secure location. Not... in a *fortress*.

We come to a stop right near the gate. Movement from the right-hand side of the car draws my attention. Two of the Shadow Monsters are moving quickly toward us, mouths gaping open, eye sockets sunken, arms filthy and covered in dried blood and mud. One of them is half-rotten with a hole ripped out of his side, the bottom rib visible. I almost gag at the sight.

His head suddenly jerks sideways, then his body flops to the ground from the momentum. He lands in a ditch and doesn't move. Damaging the brain or decapitation are the best ways to kill them once and for all.

I glance up to the fence and spot a sniper with a rifle. The second monster goes down just as fast. It's easy when there are only a few...but facing several hundred at once is a different story.

I crossed a swarm once, caught off-guard as they poured out of the woods near a river I had been bathing in. They left me alone, but being invisible to them meant they shoved and pushed and stamped over me when I fell over. I don't even know how I survived, but that was the day I decided my shelter had to be in the trees.

A crow swoops down to the ground and hops over to the dead. It pokes at a wound on the man's side, then flutters off in an instant. Not even scavengers will eat the plagued.

The gates slide open and we are on the move again. I glance back as the doors shut quickly with a final sounding clink.

We drive along a curvy road that takes us farther up the mountain, and the more distance we cover, the more my chest clenches. Pine trees coat the hill in every direction, and amid them I notice wolves roaming about. Their heavy coats of black and gray are matted, and their lips curl dangerously over sharp teeth at our presence as we drive past.

At the top of the hill lies the fortress. An oversized drawbridge lowers in front of us and we drive inside before finally coming to a stop in a large cobblestone courtyard. Half a dozen other vehicles are parked here.

The two shifters climb out of the car swiftly. My stomach tightens as Lucien approaches and lets me out.

As I climb out, he takes my hand instead of the rope binding my wrists, then he moves with fast steps away from the vehicle. Gorgeous floral and fruit trees pepper the area, and they feel so out of place. Stone houses that resemble smaller versions of castles surround the court. We walk past them, and I note lanes darting between them to more buildings behind them. There are more and more people everywhere the farther we travel. Men only... My heart is pounding wildly. Where are the women and children?

All I want to do is cry.

Everything feels foreign. All I've known for so long has been the woods and small settlements here and there with only females. But this...this place is so immense, it intimidates me.

The other shifters glance my way, eyeing me head to toe. I bristle and shy away from them, only to bump into Lucien.

"We need to go fast." There's panic in his voice, which in turn has my pulse racing.

I take a deep breath, trying to control the tremors as I push back the fear coiling inside me.

Dušan strides ahead of us, all muscles and so tall—even the way he moves is attractive. All the shifters we pass tap their fists twice to their chests as they acknowledge their Alpha.

I try to remind myself of whom I'm dealing with now. Gone is my assumption that he's just a normal shifter. This is Dušan. The Alpha whom I've heard so many horrible rumors about. I haven't exactly seen that side of him yet, if I exclude the arrogance, dominance, and kidnapping. But as he looks back at me, I worry I might get to meet that monster very soon.

At the end of the yard stands a gigantic building comparable with a castle. It's made of sand colored stone and has three towers attached to it, with pointy roofs and numerous arched windows. A large balcony encircles the top third floor. Guards stand out the front as more male shifters are pouring out of their homes, many of them sniffing the air and staring at me with too much interest. The guards' expressions reminds me of the shifter in the woods who attacked me.

Panic chokes me as we quicken our stride.

The guards step aside, and Dušan pushes open the metal door so we can enter the castle. It's dimly lit inside, the walls stone and barren of any paintings or decorations. A grand staircase with black, curled railings sits ahead of us. There is an empty feeling about the place, and it's only when I look closely at the details that I see the claw marks on the stone walls and floor. The dent in the staircase banister. Three claw marks even streak the ceiling where a candle chandelier hangs.

Dušan pauses near the mahogany staircase and swings around to face us. Heat flares over me at the way his gaze slides over me, his stunning eyes blazing with fire. It seems he can't decide on what to do with me.

"What's going to happen now?" I ask.

He doesn't respond right away, and I see the wheels spinning behind those pale blue eyes. Does he remember how I offered him shelter from the undead, how he held me tight during the night? Just when I think he might ask me to join him, he walks away and tosses over his shoulder, "Take her to the others in the waiting room." He climbs the stairs two at a time. Heaviness sinks through me, dragging me lower and lower.

Bastard.

I open my mouth to say something, but Lucien is there, taking my elbow and leading me away.

"What's in the waiting room?" I ask.

"Just a place to relax and feel safe. You don't have to worry, Meira. No one will hurt you here."

I blink at this handsome man who walks me down a dimly lit cobblestone hallway. I don't even bother trying to remember the paths we take. How far will I get if I try to escape this castle with all the guards we pass? Muscular shifters dressed in all black watch our every move.

"That's not true, is it?" I answer. "It's where I'll wait until you fly me to the Alpha I'm being traded to."

He looks over to me but says nothing because I'm right. I sigh and tear my attention away from him. My insides are like tar, sticking to my ribs, and I just want to scream.

Lucien leads me to a door at the end of the hall, his steps heavy, matching his breaths.

The door creaks open and we're facing another guard, whose eyes meet mine. He's tanned with the sides of his head shaved. A healed scar runs across his nose and under an eye.

"The missing one?" He grunts.

Lucien nods. "First flight in the morning."

His words are like daggers, jamming into my back and twisting. I'm being sent away so quickly. I'm not ready to leave. I've lived in this country my whole life. I know these woods and the monsters in them.

Lucien turns to me and fiddles with the rope around my wrists. "Dušan has an agreement with every trading pack to ensure each female he sends is never harmed."

He draws the rope free from my wrists, but he captures my hands before I can pull away. He smiles at me, as if I ought to be grateful. But I am torn up. Scared. Angry. Confused.

"A captive is still a captive," I murmur.

He looks at me with an ache sliding over his face. Those steel-gray eyes seem to pierce right into my soul as his thumb brushes against the inside of my wrist. I swallow hard.

"If you get hurt, find a way to contact us," he points out. "We check in regularly with the packs and the women. Trust me on this."

Remaining under his gaze easily sways me out of my turbulent thoughts and leaves me at his mercy. The way his thumbs stroke my wrists ignites a heady feeling that overwhelms me along with his Alpha power.

My heart racing, I stare at him like there's more between us, but that's me skating on ice without knowing how thin it is. It's reckless and can only end badly for me. All male shifters want one thing —to claim a female and impregnate her. And I can't be that woman and bring a child into this horrible world. I shouldn't want to do anything with Dušan or Lucien.

His mouth parts to explain something, but I don't want to hear any excuse he has to give me. I'll be gone tomorrow and will never see him again. I draw my hands out of his and walk into the room, leaving him behind.

There is no reason for me to trust any of these Ash Wolves. Not now or ever.

At least half a dozen women I don't recognize lounge in the room, reading books or chatting. To my surprise they seem semi-happy with being here. Two sit by the fire talking, while a brunette sits alone near the window, staring out at the forest down below. All the couches are taken, and no one looks my way. Similar to the girls on the aircraft, these are a similar age to me, dressed in clean clothes with no rips or stains.

Fighting back a tear, I crouch in the far corner and rub at the soreness in my wrists from the ropes.

I don't know how much time passes when the brunette from the window stands to stretch her back and makes her way over to me.

"How are you doing?" She sits in front me, her legs crossed.

"I hate this place," I respond.

She half-laughs and nods. "I don't get how some of them can look so relaxed." She points her chin to the girls giggling on the couch. "I'm bouncing on my toes wanting to get moving already." She talks at a million miles a minute, her hands animated. She's wearing a yellow and white stripped dress with short sleeves. Not a single smudge of dirt.

"I'm Sam," she says, running a hand through her locks. She's beautiful with the longest lashes, and she's wearing a rosy lipstick. I've only ever seen Jaine wear lipstick. She let me try it on once, only it felt sticky on my lips.

"Meira," I admit, figuring there's no need to hide it any longer. It won't change my situation.

"You're doing well, Meira, to not be freaking out. Most women just brought in don't cope well at all and have a meltdown."

"Oh, I had my moment to freak out when Dušan caught me in the woods."

Her jaw drops open. "The Alpha himself? No way!" Her voice squeals with excitement. "What's he like? I've heard so many stories, all conflicting. A couple of the women have seen him and say he looks like a god. But he won't talk to anyone less than Alpha status."

I almost choke on my laughter. "He's more a prick, if you ask me." Just saying the words takes me back to us in my treehouse and his erection poking me in the ass. Yep, he's a prick, all right.

She looks almost offended by my words at first. "What's he like? Handsome?"

I blink at her. "You haven't seen him?"

She shakes her head. "Been three days since I was captured by a male Beta and brought here. All of us girls are going to a mating ceremony tonight to see if our soulmate is in the Ash Wolves' pack. If they're not, then we will be traded to another pack somewhere in Europe. Dušan has a few trade partnerships set up apparently."

I have no clue what the ceremony entails, but I get the gist enough to make sense of what will be going down. In truth, I hate the idea of the whole damn thing. "And you're okay with this ceremony thing?"

She nods enthusiastically. "I was in heat when I hid in the woods for the past two cycles and it caused me excruciating pain. My wolf is crying out for a mate and if I stay out there, a wild shifter will hunt me down and rut me until I die. So I'm excited to finally stop running and being scared. And I can't wait to see if my mate is in this pack." She reaches out and grabs my hand, her touch almost shaky from adrenaline. "I hear Dušan and even his Third, Lucien, might be attending. Both still have to find a mate." The glint of excitement gleams in her eyes.

I can't think of anything worse. But I don't hate the woman for her happiness, if that's what she wants. "Good luck with getting an Alpha."

Her face beams. "Are you not excited about tonight?"

I stare at the women around us. Most talking are just as excited as Sam. These females crave a mate. They want a shifter to join with and to have babies. I can't imagine living like this, to let someone else control me, to no longer feel free. Mama always said that until my wolf come out, I ought to keep away from other wolves because they will kill me for being different. Which is why I fight for my freedom so much.

"You're being traded without a ceremony?" she asks.

Sighing, I say, "Yep. I'm being treated like an animal." Bitterness coats my words at remembering being caught in the woods and tossed into a truck. There, a male shifter interrogated me and made notes about me in his notebook. Then, I was hauled onto an aircraft. So while these girls get a ceremony, I got nothing like that.

"Oh, Meira." She lays a hand on my bent knee. "You're looking at this all wrong. You're gaining a life partner so you won't be alone anymore. Don't you want that?"

I shake my head, and her eyes widen at my response. "Really?" she asks.

"Don't you want more than just serving a man and having his children?" I try to keep the bitterness out of my words and not crush her dreams.

She blinks, staring at me with confusion. How nice it must be to live such an ignorant life. Maybe I'm the problem, fighting the primal call of my wolf, except I'm not like Sam or the other girls in the room. Things can never be that simple for me. What lies inside me isn't normal, but I push those thoughts away.

"Well, Meira," Sam says as she stands. "I'm sorry you get traded and don't get a chance to find your soulmate in this pack first. We wolves are all born to find our other half, not to be loners, so I will say a prayer to the moon that you will find your mate soon." With a short smile, she strolls across the room to join the others on the couch.

I lower my head and stare at the wooden floor, noting the scratch marks. Sam's words stay with me. Except I remind myself I'm not like her, and the only solution for me is to be on my own.

Time passes as I close my eyes and drift off into sleep. Now, it's night outside, and with it comes a lingering pain across my middle. It gets stronger, slicing deeper through me.

I push myself to my feet. Maybe walking will ease the ache. No one pays me any attention, but all I can think about is breathing slow and pushing past the pain. It always comes and goes. My sickness has never left me, even after all these nineteen years.

But the pain lashes over me as if someone whipped me. I cry out, clutching my stomach, and then fall to my knees.

Voices escalate around me. Someone is at my side, but I can't focus on anything. I hiss with the laceration tearing through me. It deepens, getting sharper, closing in around my stomach.

"Meira," Sam says, frantically waving at someone behind me.

I drop to the floor. Stars blink in my eyes, blurring my sight. My gut is on fire, feeling like someone is scooping out my insides. I hug myself, drawing my knees to my chest as I try to deal with the excruciating pain.

"I need help..." The words tear from my mouth as darkness feathers at the edges of my vision.

CHAPTER 7

DUŠAN

The Alpha in me demands I call Ander and confirm that I found his missing Omega. Except my wolf snarls with venom at the thought of not claiming her myself. That delicious mouth of hers says so many things she shouldn't—words that I've punished other wolves for. I ought to drag her aside and spank that tight little ass for her comments back in the woods.

That doesn't stop me from wanting to fuck her so hard the whole settlement hears her cry out in pleasure and knows she's been claimed. That she's mine. All those male shifters staring at her hungrily in the courtyard riled me up, and now I need to take care of that annoyance. She's an unmarked female, and her scent is ripe, calling males to her. Except for a true mating to happen, her wolf must accept the male.

I sigh and lean over the balcony outside my office, the wind still today, but I feel something brewing in the energy. Below, the evergreen pine forest stretches across the mountain. The old Râșnov city sits nearby, now abandoned and decayed. No one lives there aside from the occasional squatters. The streets are filled with undead, so humans left long ago.

Someone clears their throat, and I inhale Lucien's woodsy wolf scent as he joins me outside. "There's something different about her."

I know exactly whom he's talking about. I saw the look in his eyes when he first met Meira, the hitch of his breath, the acceleration of his heart. She's taken me like an unsuspecting storm, her scent refusing to leave me, her fiery attitude a challenge I want to accept.

I face my Third and school my thoughts on business. "Ander is expecting her delivery."

He bobs his head, but I don't miss the tightness around his eyes. "What if we hold on to her a while longer?" he suggests. "Discover what makes her different. I doubt Ander will appreciate us sending him faulty goods."

The wind drives his brown hair off his face, and he grips the railing alongside me.

"She's affected you that much?" I ask.

Steel-gray eyes raise to meet mine. "Not a fucking chance."

I almost believe him. Almost. He's always been able to convince others he's not impacted by the state of the world, as if he's immovable as a mountain, and that he just pushes on when life gets tough. But I know the man who stands before me. He's a friend who lost so fucking much that the only way to cope is to embrace denial. There's a reason he wears cowboy boots. They are the only thing he has left of his father, so he isn't as good at hiding his pain as he thinks.

"Mad and Caspian need to fucking return from the X-Clan." I growl. "I don't need a hothead like Mad ruining my trade agreements by doing something stupid." My shoulders stiffen. The only way I keep everyone in my pack safe is with this exchange. Delivering Meira fixes the problem. So why do doubts sweep through my mind about sending her to Ander?

My wolf snorts at my indecision. If he could laugh, he'd be howling. Wolves are meant to be mated. It's how we're built.

Wearing an irksome smirk, Lucien claps me on the back. "She's gotten to you too, I see."

"Fuck." I shake my head. "I don't need this." Pushing a hand through my hair, I stare out over the landscape. "There's something wrong with her. Her scent isn't right." And if I'd met my mate, I'd know. Which is why I think what I'm feeling is little more than lust.

"Part of me wonders if she isn't a cross between different wolf breeds," Lucien suggests.

I meet his stare, my gaze narrowing. "You think she's from an opposing pack?"

He shrugs. "You once told me to never dismiss any possibility."

Except she lived out in that treehouse. Well, at least, I thought she did. Doesn't mean she can't be aligned with another pack. There are many breeds of wolf shifters, many ready to kill and get their hands on my pack and territory. Kill me, and they have the right to fight for the spot of Alpha to my pack.

I grit my teeth and suck in a sharp breath, trying to control myself. She couldn't be a spy to let Alphas into the pack? But do I really know her?

Footsteps draw my attention behind me, ripping me from my thoughts.

Mihai is in the office, and I nod. Perfect. I'm about to find out exactly what happened with the delivery to X-Clan Wolves.

Lucien and I walk the length of the balcony and step inside to join Mihai.

Mihai double-taps his chest before bowing his head. He's a Beta and charged with managing my transportation and has been doing a damn good job for years. But Mad quickly blamed him for Meira missing from the delivery.

"Dušan," he says, as he waits for a command.

"Sit."

He does so across the desk from me. The rest of the room is empty. This isn't a place to lounge in—it's a place to get shit done. Lucien stands by the doorway to the balcony, his shadow stretching out over Mihai. He sits still, his back straight, never cowering.

"You've never let me down," I begin. "So, how did a girl go missing on the last delivery?"

He takes a deep breath, followed by a few moments of uncomfortable silence. Mihai's gaze slides from Lucien to me. "I delivered nine girls." He fiddles with something in his pocket and pulls out a folded-up piece of paper. Placing it in front of me, he unfolds it.

I read the list of girls, with the last one being Meira. Each has a tick on them, as per all other delivery slips. We've never had this problem before.

Looking up, I don't see a wolf who looks like he's hiding something. The telltale signs of lying aren't there; neither is he nervous sweating.

"So, you sure nine girls got on that aircraft?"

His eyes hold mine, never once looking away. "I supplied them to Mad at the plane like I always do, then I left. I didn't do a damn thing different."

Without Mad here, I can't corroborate either story. But I do have Meira, who has no reason to lie about how she escaped. The only problem is getting her to open up.

"And Mad?" Lucien asks. "Anything different about his behavior?"

Mihai barks a laugh. "Mad was his usual prick self, telling me to fuck off because they were running late."

I blink at him, unaware of the flight being delayed. So, from what I gather, the girls arrived at the aircraft. Except somehow, Mad lost one between loading them up and taking off, since Meira was still in our woods and not two countries away. I don't need fuck-ups. I glance over to my video com and reach for it to call Mad.

"Excuse me." Jay, one of my close guards, abruptly sticks his head into my office. Panic crawls over his face. "I'm sorry for barging in, but we have an emergency."

"What is it?" I snarl.

"Something's wrong with the new female wolf. She was crying from pain and just passed out."

My heart clenches. Lucien steps closer, his breaths quickening.

"Bring her to my room," I order.

I stare at Lucien incredulously after our discussion that something is different about her. Mihai, still in his seat, furrows his brow in confusion.

"You can go," I tell him. "We'll discuss this later."

Meira

My eyes fly open, and my heart races. Sweat rolls down the sides of my face and neck, my whole body flaring with heat. I squint against the sunlight pouring into the room from the arched window. I don't know where I am at first. Slowly my surroundings come into view.

Stone walls remind me I'm in a castle with the Ash Wolves. A soft bed is beneath me as I lie on my side staring at a wardrobe made of dark timber, the corners carved ornately with wolves howling at the moon. There's a lush rug the color of fresh blood on the floor. I haven't seen anything so clean and new for a long time.

I smell him all over the bed. Dušan. His musky and wolf scent floods me, just as it did back in my treehouse. This is his room. The Alpha has placed me in his bed, which confuses me, considering he abruptly left me to be sent to the waiting room for shipping out.

"How are you feeling?" a deep voice asks from behind me.

I roll over to find Lucien sitting on the edge of the bed, looking at me with concern.

"You had us all scared when you passed out and wouldn't wake."

"My throat is dry," I croak, glancing around the room and finding a black leather lounge chair against the window.

Lucien reaches over to the bedside table next to him and picks up a glass of water.

I blink at him and shuffle to sit upright in bed. That familiar ache pulses through me. My sickness has come at me harder than before, the pain excruciating. What is going on with me? My stomach tightens because letting these wolves see me this sick will do me no favors. It will get me cast to the bottom of their pack hierarchy... too broken to be anything other than their slave.

He hands me the full glass. Our fingers brush, and a jolt of energy dances up my arm. It spreads through me and overwhelms me with a scorching heat. I lose my breath and swallow hard, trying to push past the sensation that draws me to this Alpha. Everything about him consumes me. Part of me wants to give in, to ask him to protect me. Another part hates those thoughts, but my body betrays me.

When I lift my gaze to him, I see his wolf stirring behind those stunning steel-gray eyes. The ones I want to fall into and get lost in.

I mentally shake myself, needing distance away from these Alphas.

"I'm feeling better," I lie as I drink down the icy water, chasing the heat that clings to me.

He looks at me as though he stares right into my soul. I hand back the empty glass and smile, fighting back the pain that leaves me groggy and exhausted. Normally, I'd stay in bed a few days to wait for the sickness to pass, but I've lost that luxury.

"Are you sick?" he asks, refusing to let go of the topic. Of course, he won't.

I shake my head. "Hadn't eaten for a while. I think it was just hunger pains."

He nods, but the way he studies me makes it clear he doesn't believe me. "We suspected that, so I gave you a small injection that should help."

My gaze instinctively goes to my arms and I look down at a small bandage on the inside of my elbow. I try not to overthink what he gave me, not wanting him to suspect me of panicking. But I have no clue how that will impact my illness.

With the small towel in his hand, he reaches over and moistens my brow. There's a tenderness in his strokes, in the way he looks at me.

Yet panic crawls up my spine.

"It's a bit hot in here," I say jokingly, but he isn't smiling.

I blink hard, and my thoughts seem to stutter.

"Don't worry. The injection was nothing more than vitamins to help boost your immune system."

Is that all it really was?

"And why am I in Dušan's bed?" The room has a warmth to it, a coziness, and it's been a long time since I felt this way. Sleeping on splintered logs can never replace the softness of a mattress.

"He insisted on it as soon as he heard you had passed out." Lucien is on his feet. "Let me get you some food."

When he turns to leave, I ask, "How long have I been sleeping for?"

"Two full days without waking."

I quickly steel myself and half-laugh, as I usually sleep for several days, which isn't normal by any standard. "I was clearly exhausted."

"Yeah, that must be it." He walks out and shuts the door, and the click of a lock resonates through the room.

Shit! I collapse back down in bed, my body throttling with pain. Curling in on myself, I bury my face in the pillow and want to cry.

Fear shakes me. This is why I avoided being caught for so long. The sickness makes me vulnerable, so how long before Dušan realizes this and works out that I've never shifted into my wolf? I've never been able to be whole. I'll be cast aside, and not even those starved males will want to touch me. I'll be locked up because someone like me shouldn't exist.

I draw the blanket to my chest and clasp my eyes shut, praying for the aches to leave. Then I'm finding a way out of here.

On the bright side, I didn't get shipped out to the other pack. Maybe that's a good omen. I ignore the mocking laughter in my head and cling on to the last threads of hope I have left.

Lucien

The color of her bronze eyes reminds me of blazing fire. They stay with me, refusing to leave my mind. As does her heady scent, along with the smell of blood. I can't work it out, but she is definitely hiding something. Any other shifter and I'd have forced the answers out of them by now. But Meira does something to me. My beast calms in my chest, but she makes me anxious. Secrets get you killed in this world, so what secrets is the little wolf keeping?

I find myself standing outside the door to the

bedroom she's in, like I don't have control of my own actions because my wolf insists I stay near. When she touched my hand, a buzz shot up my arm, slamming into me. She stole my breath away... My body went tight, and my wolf pressed forward as I curled my fists. An automatic reaction to protect her overwhelmed me.

Shock filled her eyes, and I burned to reach across the bed and take her into my arms. All I could think about was how beautiful she was, how I needed to taste her lips.

Fuck! My head is a heaping mess.

I still feel her presence. Now I understand Dušan's response to keep her safe in his bedroom, of all places. He feels what I do around Meira. Except, I've never heard of there being two or more soulmates for a wolf.

I push from her door and still feel the pull as I walk away. From deep inside, my wolf surges forward, aching for the shift.

Meira.

He calls to her, but I can't allow myself to want her. She'll be sent away, and if she doesn't, my Alpha gets first pick and first decision if he'll share.

As Third to the Alpha of Ash Wolves, I can't lose my head. Especially not when the Second is a fucking idiot. It frustrates me that Dušan keeps Mad in such a role, when this isn't the first time shit went south from his involvement. Just because he's his step-brother doesn't mean he's deserving of the role.

Clenching my fists, I march outside and weave between the homes until I reach the edge of the fortress, ready to scream. Sucking in fresh air, I try to calm my racing pulse.

My head roars, while my heart yearns for Meira.

Great way to keep my head screwed on straight.

"Lucien," a male calls from behind me.

With a deep sigh, I turn to find Chase greeting me with a bow. He's a Beta who manages all festivities and pack runs. He's not a large shifter by any means, but his devotion to the pack is unchallenging.

"Everything ready for tonight?" I ask.

"Yes. I wanted to show you where we set up the circuit for the races. Make sure you approve."

The circuit is used for the younger wolves, the newly turned who aren't ready to run with the Alphas through the woods within the settlement.

He has a heart of gold, and even being in his

late twenties, he lacks the confidence to make his own decisions. "You know what? I'll trust you."

He gazes at me with concern in his eyes.

I laugh and slap him on the shoulder. "You've done this how many times already?"

"At least a dozen," he says.

"Well, then under your guidance, this will be the greatest one yet."

He steadies himself and gives a nod. Then he's gone. I turn back to looking out to the Carpathian Mountains ahead of me.

Meira won't leave my thoughts. But I never expected any female to ever affect me in such a way. After losing my mate, Cataline, I shattered into hundreds of pieces and vowed to never find love again.

CHAPTER 8

DUŠAN

I stare at my Fourth. "She may be an Omega, but there's more to her."

Bardhyl nods. "I've never heard of a wolf being sick like this before, except for Omegas who are in pain from their heat cycle. But not vomiting blood."

My body definitely responds around Meira's body, and my wolf insists we claim her. Her presence draws me with such compelling energy.

None of the other Omegas I've met have shown the symptoms Meira has during heat—bedridden and looking physically ill with pasty skin.

"Could she be carrying a virus? A precursor to becoming an undead?" I ask, my gut tightening at the thought that if she is, I'll have to get rid of her.

Bardhyl thinks about it for a second. He's from Denmark and looks every bit like his Viking ancestors... sandy blond hair worn loose over his shoulders. He's a warrior at heart and looks like one, towering over most. He's fierce and will never back away from a battle, which is one of the reasons he's on my team.

"Doubt it," he answers. "Otherwise, you'd show signs of being sick after the time you spent with her, and I've never seen an undead infection take this long to take over a new host."

"I guess," I say. We both stride along the outside of the fortress, my head trying to make sense of what we're dealing with. "I keep running every possible scenario through my head. Like she can't be a half-breed, or she'd be dead already at her age. So that can't be it."

The forest descends away from the fortress and goes all the way down to the metal fence, where there are more wolves running around in the woods.

"The blood sample Lucien took from Meira is still with our lab," he explains. "We're lacking all the technologies to do extensive testing, so it's just going to take a bit."

A black wolf darts through the woods inside

the fence, followed by four others. As our pack grows, the space becomes limited for shifters needing freedom.

Bang. Bang.

I look over to the front gate, at the guards in the tower, taking out the approaching undead.

"There're more and more lately," Bardhyl says. "It's like something is calling them here."

I cut him a look, because I've had the same thought. For weeks now, the infected have appeared more frequently around our perimeter. "Can you look into that?"

He gives a quick nod, and his shoulders broaden. "I'm going down there," my Fourth says, then he lunges into a sprint down the hill—while I turn and march back into the fortress to pay Meira another visit.

Two nights. That's how long I've slept in the spare room, and each time I go into my bedroom, Meira is fast asleep, so what exactly is going on with that hellcat? I need to talk to her, so she better be awake.

There's no way I can send her to Ander in this state, so I've avoided calling him until I understand what I'm dealing with. Part of me wonders if I should swallow my pride and promise Ander a different female. He'll know no matter what... We send him a full spec sheet of every female we deliver.

I seethe at the idea of not keeping my word, since that doesn't make for a very trusting business relationship. We may be from different packs and wolf species, but at the core, we aren't too dissimilar. Which means my inability to deliver what I initially promised is a strike against our growing business partnership. I can't afford for the X-Clan Wolves to have any doubts about dealing with me. All the pack members under my care depend on me supplying medicine and technologies to better protect us and to hunt down food.

Morning sunlight pours through the arched window of the steadfast castle as I stride through its corridors, only the echo of my boots striking the cobblestone floor resonates through the fortress.

I push open my bedroom door and walk straight in out of pure habit, then halt, guilt punching me in the gut from just barging in here.

Meira is bowed over my trashcan, heaving into it.

I cross the room in three strides. "Meira, are you okay?"

She wipes the back of her mouth and straightens herself, meeting my gaze. Her eyes are watery, as if she's been crying.

Steeling her posture, she tries to smile, only I see the pain she's in. "I feel better now," she admits.

My chest tightens at seeing her in agony. I'll never forgive myself if she dies while under my care. I reach down and take her hand. It's clammy to the touch. "I know exactly what you need."

"Yeah, what's that?" she croaks, trying her best to act normal, but I can see right through her lie.

"You'll see." I take her with me, but not before I take a quick look into the trashcan and see blood.

Fuck! She's really sick… except, I don't understand *why*.

"Thank you," she says, distracting me from my thoughts. "Guess I'm just not used to living indoors."

Her excuse is almost laughable, but I let her have her moment. She doesn't have the strength to defend herself, and if I push, she'll grumble. So I say nothing and focus on her healing first.

She walks strong and tall, but her hair is damp and stuck to her head. This isn't the girl I found in the woods, but a shadow of her.

It isn't long before we reach the baths, located at the end of a hall on the ground floor. We step through an arched doorway and before us lies a large sunken bath large enough to fit ten shifters. Steam rises from its surface, and heat greets us as we walk inside. The water ripples from the regular filtering. Without the solar panels I traded with the X-Clan for energy—for things like keeping this bath constantly warm and clean—we'd still be living in the dark ages.

"Wow!" Meira's eyes grow in size as she pulls her hand free from mine and steps closer to the edge of the stone bath. At the back are the saunas and bathrooms, but right now, there's no one here but the two of us.

"A bath will help relax your anxiety," I suggest, hoping this will help her to start trusting me and eventually open up to me.

She looks over to me, her expression heartfelt, like she expected me to throw her into a dungeon. Even when she's sick and looks like death, there's an aching digging in my gut to claim her. Her presence alone drives me insane.

"You're going to watch me have a bath?" She arches a brow.

I laugh, because I'm not going anywhere. "The

toilet and shower are in the back. I'll have a hot drink brought to you."

Meira nods and turns to the bath without a word. There's only one way in and out of the room, so she isn't escaping without going past me first.

I march out of the baths and head down the hall, finally tracking down a bulky guard.

"Send word to the kitchen to take a tray of peppermint tea and fresh bread slices to Meira in the baths. Also, speak to Alyna about finding a dress for her, and ensure no one enters the baths until I come out, understand?"

"Of course." He bows and marches down the corridor.

I walk in the opposite direction, taking long strides. I'm ready to find out everything I can about this shifter girl and what exactly her secret is.

By the time I return, Meira has her back to me, completely naked and stepping into the bath. My gaze slides over her shoulders, her tiny waist, and to a perfectly curved ass before she dips into the water all the way to her neck.

The image goes straight to my cock. I step

forward. "Warm enough?" I ask, my throat suddenly thick.

She turns abruptly in the water toward me, her eyes wide. The shadowy outline of her body reveals itself below the surface in ripple effect as a gentle wave washes over her breasts.

She gasps. "Why are you in here?"

"It's a communal bath."

Her attention flips to the doorway and back, her arms lashing over her breasts. "So you're just going to stand there and watch me?"

"Would you prefer if I join you?"

"No!" Her response flies past her lips, and I laugh loudly at her nervousness. She doesn't realize how much that innocence affects me.

I stroll across the room, feeling her eyes on me. The restroom is a tiny room with two toilet cubicles, three showers, and a few sinks. I find her clothes piled on the floor, then I collect soap from the sink and a fresh towel from the rack. Back in the room, she's pressed into the corner of the bath, looking unsure of herself. I set the soap down in front of her as she looks up at me with those spectacular pale bronze eyes. She's searching for something in me, expecting something I don't understand.

"How are you feeling?" I ask.

"The water is soothing. I don't feel so sick anymore."

"Good," I murmur as I take a seat on a wooden bench alongside the bath and set a towel down beside me. Stretching my feet out, crossing them at the ankle, I recline and watch my hellcat. "You'd better get to washing or I'm climbing in there and washing you myself."

"You wouldn't dare," she hisses, her brows pulling together. Damn, she's sexy when she's angry.

I arch a brow and lean forward, my elbows resting against my thighs. "Is that a challenge?"

Her glare is like tossing daggers my way.

"Yeah, that's what I thought."

She clicks her tongue, and a mischievous expression slides over her face. Snatching the soap, she drags it under the water.

"So let's talk," I say. "What was going on? Are you injured, is that why you're sick?"

She shakes her head. "No, I'm not sick. I'm just having a hard time acclimatizing."

That's why she vomited blood? Right.

Someone clears their throat outside the bath, and I sniff the air. A timber-like smell... the guard.

I jolt to my feet and find him waiting outside the entrance, carrying a tray filled with food and a midnight blue dress hanging off his arm. I reach over and rip off the store tag. We often do trips out to the old human cities to find clothing for our pack.

"Thank you," I say as I collect them from him.

"Will that be all?" There's a quirk at the corners of his lips. He's likely imagining that I want to be alone with Meira. Except my intentions are purely to find out information, even if my wolf insists something completely different is going on.

I nod. "Just keep watch so no one barges in."

"Of course."

With fast steps, I return to the bath, where Meira is starting to climb out. But the moment she sees me, she dips back in. Sneaky minx.

"These should help settle your stomach." I set the tray near the edge of the steaming bath.

I take a seat and place her dress on top of the towel. "So, you were telling me something about acclimatization making you sick?"

She glares at me and suddenly submerges herself under the water, then pushes back up. Her dark hair is slicked back, her face radiant and eyes full. Gone is the look of pained sickness from her expression. The woman in front of me is the one I caught in the woods.

Helping herself to the tea, she draws the cup into the middle of the bath with her, sipping away, her eyes never leaving me.

"Not sure what to tell you. Just had a bad couple of days. We all have them."

"Well, that's the thing, Meira." I study the way the corner of her eyes twitch with concern. "Wolves don't get sick," I say. "We're not built that way, and the only sickness to ever impact our kind has been the virus spread from a bite by an undead. But you…" I fold my arms over my chest. "*You* are sick with something else. How?"

She presses the cup to her lips and takes her time drinking it before returning the empty cup to the edge of the bath and moving to the shallower part of the pool. Her shoulders glide out of the water as she starts to lather herself with the soap.

"There's only one reason a wolf could be sick like this," I say.

Her gaze cuts over to me, fierceness flaring behind her eyes. "Don't know what to tell you. Maybe you're reading too much into it. Both my parents were wolves."

She pushes herself farther up to where the

water cascades to her waist, exposing her breasts... the perfectly round and perky globes tipped with a deep cherry nipple.

My thoughts dissolve at the sight. Intoxicating. Fuckable. Dangerous.

She is perfection, and this beauty will haunt me for eternity. I never expected this from her. Those perfect full breasts are driving me wild.

I see right through what she's doing, but I can't stop my thoughts from falling prey. My wolf shoves forward, wanting to claim her. The spark in me flares awake, filling the emptiness I've lived with for so many years. I've bedded dozens of women, but none have touched me this way. None have roused my wolf to such a state of reckless lust.

Looking at her, I want it all. Every stroke, every taste, every desire. To be cock deep inside her, to make her cry out with pleasure, for her to be mine.

A growl flares from me as she lifts the soap and washes her arms and chest with a thick lather.

I can't look away. My cock punches against my pants, my breath hitches. I didn't expect her to be this conniving. She surprises me.

Her hands slide slowly and deliberately up and over her breasts. They jiggle with each movement, hypnotizing me. Her breasts bounce, the soft peaks hardening against their soapy coating.

Fuck me! She's teasing me, making a small moaning sound that goes straight to my dick. I can't breathe as a savage arousal rips through me.

"What were we talking about again?" she murmurs, like she's forgotten.

She's devious and manipulative. But has to be in order to survive in this world, and I'm enjoying her trying to distract me. My mind runs away with me as I picture myself pressing into her and filling her.

Her fingers dance under her breasts and over her narrow waist before dipping lower under the water. I ball my hands, digging blunt fingernails into my palms to stop from lunging forward and taking what I crave. Her eyes glint with mischief as she narrows them toward me. I try to stay still, to hold back, but it grows harder and harder.

"Wolf," I growl. "You're playing in dangerous waters."

She smirks and splashes me before dunking herself completely under the surface of the water.

A snarl abruptly escapes my lips.

I'm on my feet before I can stop myself,

standing at the edge of the bath, drawn to her. Needing her.

She explodes back out of the water, shoving the water off her face, soapy bubbles running down her gorgeous body.

When she sees me so close, she blinks rapidly, forcing herself backward through the bath. Panic flares over her face, and my pulse is raging with the chase.

Darkness stretches over my mind.

Need drives into my gut. What spell has she put on me? She stares at me with fear… a fear that has my balls drawing up tighter, hurting like fuck for release.

My muscles tense, I watch her wade through the bath and hurry out. Her gaze scans the bathroom, then she spots the towel on the bench, closer to her.

She turns toward it, and I drink in her scorching hot body. The small bounce in her breasts with each step, the tight stomach, the thatch of black hair between her legs.

Water drips down her body. I want her legs splayed open, to taste her, lick her, sink my teeth into her and take what's mine.

She moves quickly, but I'm faster, at her side in a second.

She gasps and backs away.

I press my hands to the stone wall at her back, caging her in. I inhale her slick desire, still unable to pin down her scent. But it doesn't matter to my wolf, who rumbles in my chest. I look down at her naked body, my cock straining against my pants. I groan beneath my breath at the way she stares at me, and holding myself back grows harder.

She's spectacular.

"You drive me insane with desire," I snarl. "My wolf pines for you, but there's so much more to you, isn't there?" I try to shake the fog out of my head, to think straight. "All I can think about is fucking you until you scream my name."

"Y-You w-want to mark me?" she whispers, her words shaky.

Meira

He steps back and turns away from me, leaving me breathless. His words and actions affect me more than I should let them. No man has ever spoken to me this way. Yet I don't back away, but instead, shiver with fear...with *need*. My wolf whimpers inside me, wanting to give Dušan everything we have. Except he's too close to the truth...

No wolf wants an impure shifter.

I will die before I give in to an Alpha or any male who wants me for nothing but slavery.

"Get dressed," he orders with his back to me.

My heart flutters with anxiety and my cheeks blush as I grab the blue dress on the bench and drag it down over my head. It cinches in around my waist and sits tightly over my chest. It has long, flowing sleeves and a skirt that dances around my knees.

"What do you want from me?" I growl. "I don't want to be here. Tell me how *you* would feel if you were ripped away from your life and forced to be a slave?"

He spins toward me fast, his eyes narrowing. "That's what you think this is? Being in a safe settlement is slavery? Then I've been a fool to think I was helping you."

My mouth drops open. "You plan to trade me to another pack, so how is that helping?"

His breaths deepen, but I won't back down to this Alpha. He lashes out and seizes my chin, forcing my head back. "You don't know what being a prisoner actually feels like. I grew up with a father who was more terrifying than the undead outside. Who fucked every female in his pack and treated everyone around him like garbage. Who killed his own kind for not following his rules. What I offer is a longer life, whether in my pack or another pack that I know will treat females right." He swallows hard and releases me. A snarl tears from his mouth as he turns away from me abruptly.

I stumble backward, my heart shackled by his words.

"How long did you really think you'd last out there alone with the rogue wolves once they caught your scent?" he asks.

"I did well enough this long," I spit back.

"You want to know what I think?" He grabs my arm and drags me toward the doorway. "I think you're afraid to live in a pack. Afraid because you're a *half-breed*."

My heart starts beating, and I stumble alongside him, my words freezing up.

"That's why you're sick. Your human side is ill."

He spins me around by the shoulders, drawing me against his chest. "You know what else your sickness tells me? You haven't had your first transformation yet, have you? Otherwise you would have shifted by now and healed from your wolf side."

I swallow painfully, looking up at him as my heart drops right through me that he's uncovered the truth. My father was human, and he met Mama when he saved her from a bear trap in the woods. He cared for her until she was conscious enough to transform and heal herself. Mama often told me it was the making of a romantic story... that was before he left us.

I lift my chin to Dušan, well aware that he doesn't know everything about me yet, but it's enough to set off alarm bells in my head. It tells me he's savvy enough to pay attention to everything I do. And that means I'm in trouble if I stay much longer in this settlement. What will he do when he discovers why the undead don't attack me? There is no way he can find out because I won't become anyone's lab experiment.

"What will you do to me?" I ask.

"That's up to you." He cocks his head to the side, staring at me sharply.

I blink at him, confused.

"You can stay as you are and keep getting sicker until you die. Or I can help you find a way to bring on your wolf with a forced mating." His gaze softens. He's looking at me as if he pities me.

Forced mating. The air rushes out of my lungs. After a male marks a female, she's forever under his command. Her wolf will obey him, and he owns her. Mama told me males can still mark a female with a bite that binds her to him even if they aren't fated mates. That's what lots of Alphas do, making a harem for themselves through a forced mating. So is that what Dušan wants? To keep me as his sex slave? I can't—I *won't*. I love my freedom too much to be owned by anyone. I stiffen. He will own me over my dead body.

"I'll be fine alone," I declare, as I lift my chin high, my mind stuttering and panic clutching at my chest. "My wolf will come out soon enough. I can feel her pushing, and I don't need your help."

"Half-breeds don't survive transformations on their own," he explains, his fury taming. "Maybe you need some time alone to think about your next steps. You don't have to be alone in this."

I'm lost, his words ripping over my mind. Fury punches me in the gut at his persistence, and my words come flying out. "There's a reason they don't survive. What lies inside half-breeds are monsters, not perfect wolves like you." It's what I've heard from shifters in other settlements.

He reaches for my hand. "That's not—"

"Don't," I cry out. "I don't need your sympathy or pity. I've lived with what I am for years."

The stone walls seem to close in around me. I can't settle down my nerves as I study his face. Shadows gather in his eyes and he doesn't say anything.

Because he knows what I say is the truth.

CHAPTER 9

MEIRA

I stumble into an empty room, the door shutting behind me with a clap, followed by the click of the lock.

"Fuck you, Dušan!" I yell as I spin around the empty room. Footfalls fade away outside.

"Sonofabitch!" I shout.

Four white walls, a small lamp, no window. My heart thumps wildly, and I'm drowning in so many emotions. Fear and unease uncoil within me.

He knows. He fucking knows I'm a half-breed. Half-wolf, half-human. When my kind don't transform once we hit puberty, like me, the animal inside of us changes and becomes a ruthless monster.

Old feelings flare through me, tearing at my

heart. I've been happy hiding, letting everyone believe I was an Omega, a Beta, whatever they told themselves…anything but the truth.

I tremble, hating the pity Dušan gave me when he worked out what I was…I don't need anyone's sympathy, let alone this Alpha's.

My human father left us because I wasn't good enough.

Dušan now wants to force a mating onto me because I'm not enough as I am. The idea terrifies me. What if my wolf comes out? Will I die? Will she kill everyone around her? If by some miracle I survive, and then other shifters murder her, then I'm gone too.

It's why I've stayed so long in the woods, always alone.

No wolf will accept a half-breed as a true mate. I am nothing more than an outcast and weak.

I hate the world and loathe myself.

I feel desperate, more so than I have for a long time.

I don't want to feel used. It's hard enough living with what I am, let alone having others mistreat me for it.

Tears drench my cheeks. I don't remember

starting to cry, but they fall like the broken shards of my life.

I squeeze my eyes shut, hugging myself tightly. In my mind, I see Mama in my vision from when I was younger and we had just moved into a new settlement, her face morphed into a furious frown. I had forgotten to shut the latch on the shed, and the chickens got out. They ran out of the settlement and into the woods that were crawling with undead.

I etch her face to the back of my eyelids. It has been so long since I had dreamed of her or seen her in my thoughts. Often, I lie in my treehouse for hours trying to picture her face, to remember on what side she parted her hair. But those little things fade with time.

My heart lurches like an undead. I miss her horribly. *She'd* know what I should do right now.

For so long, I have despised the world. But then what should I do? Cry myself into a puddle?

"Calm down," I scold myself. It's not as if I can control the way I was born, but what I can control is what I do with my life.

If I'm lucky, I'll be kicked out of this settlement, except I learned long ago that holding on to hope that things go my way is the quickest way to get myself killed.

I look up at the door and know exactly what I need to do.

To escape.

My sickness is tamed for now, so this is the time to move. Wiping my eyes, I stand tall, then blink at the lamp sitting in the corner, throwing light across the room.

I inspect the lamp up close before I snap off two of the metal brackets that cradle the lightbulb. They're hot to the touch, but I barely feel it when my whole body is flooded with adrenaline.

In front of the door, I lean over and jam the thin metal rods into the keyhole, twisting them left and right. Jaine taught me how to break locks, saying, *"This will save your life one day."*

A metal click sounds, and I smirk to myself as I push those two pins into my pocket then pull open the door. Quickly, I look outside. There's no one in sight.

I slip out and run along the corridor, remembering that I passed an arched passage to freedom this way. The walls are bare. Not a single painting, decoration, or rug adorns the place. The castle feels cold and nothing like a home.

A chill runs up my spine. I shoot a glance over my shoulder. No one follows, so I move faster.

Sunlight splashes the hallway ahead of me and my heart soars. I scramble up the stone steps two at a time, and swing right, following the light, bursting through the arched passage. I squint at first, adjusting to the brightness. I'm on an oversized balcony with a carved stone railing, at least three stories off the ground. Down below, the fortress grounds stretch out before me—the courtyard we walked through when I first arrived, the driveway and the metal gates. The metal fence encasing this territory shows just how enormous this settlement is.

Something creeps into my chest, a feeling I haven't felt since the last settlement I lived in with Mama. Where everything was safe and cozy. Until it wasn't.

But here, the settlement is enormous. How does Dušan control all these wolves? Where does he get the resources to feed and protect them? By the amount of homes below, there have to be close to two hundred wolves living here, maybe more. The sting in my heart pierces deeper for the simple reason that under any other circumstance, this could be a perfect home for me. Minus the small problem of me being a half-breed, putting me at the bottom of his wolf hierarchy and making me a monster in their eyes.

I need to get out of here. I swing around to find the balcony I'm standing on curls outward on either side of the castle.

Voices come from inside the building, and my heart pounds in my ears. I don't wait, running to the left, where the balcony vanishes out of sight.

Someone will see me!

Running, I breathe heavily as I push myself. Each time I pass a window, I duck to avoid being seen. I don't stop, hurrying on and praying I find some way down that doesn't involve going back indoors.

The castle is massive and I'm running out of breath by the time I reach the other end. I pause for a moment, sucking in breaths when I spot a set of metal steps a bit farther away. A desperate gasp escapes my lips.

"Someone's watching you," a male stranger hisses in my ear.

I jump in my skin from sheer fright. I jerk around, my arms raised to my chest. "Fuck!"

"Boo!"

My whole body goes rigid at the shifter in front

of me. Pale blond hair flutters over his strong, broad shoulders. He has pale skin, and his eyes are a vivid green, like he's one with the forest. The rest of him reminds of a Viking god. Built like a bear, he towers over me, dressed in jeans and a long-sleeved black tee. My knees weaken, and his presence alone leaves me utterly speechless. His closeness turns my reaction to a wash of heat.

I recoil, panic gripping me.

Seizing my arm, he hauls me toward him, my feet almost floating under me from his quickness. His eyes darken with the intensity of an Alpha, and the sensation of this power swarms me.

Face to face, his breath grazes over my brow, and my inhale hitches at his crisp wolf smell mixed with the fresh mountain air. My pounding heart leaves me breathless.

Clasping on to my bravery, I shove myself to my toes, lean closer, and kiss him right on the lips.

He flinches, not expecting that. I land a quick kick to his shin, and then rip out of his grip.

He grunts, but I'm already flying down the metal stairs, my hands sliding over the railing, my feet scrambling down so fast, I keep losing my footing.

"Get your ass back up here!" he orders.

My heart is racing. I hop down on the landing.

A heavy *thud* sounds behind me, the ground trembling.

I spin around, and he's right there, reaching out to grab me.

"Leave me alone!" I flick my arm up to block his, then pivot right out of his grasp.

He rushes up behind me, and large arms swoop around my middle, lifting me off the ground. Suddenly, my legs are flailing about midair as he has me tucked under his arm.

Irritation flushes my skin.

"Where are you running to?

My mind races. Maybe he doesn't realize who I am, so I can trick him into letting me go.

"Put me down. I'm on my way home and you startled me."

"What quadrant do you live in?" he growls, a hint of northern European accent coming through.

I sigh loud enough for effect. "Why are you grilling me? Isn't this place our sanctuary?"

He chuckles. "Why don't you come with me? I can help you out," he deadpans.

Setting me down on my feet, he drags his gaze from me to the path around the ground floor of the castle to where the houses are located. His expression is neutral, while my stomach is exploding with nervous butterflies.

I made a mistake—this gorgeous Viking definitely knows who I am. I see it in his eyes, in the slight tick in his jaw when he stares at me. He's about to take me back to Dušan.

"What's your name?" I demand to know, lifting my chin, all for bravado.

He spears a hand through his hair, narrowing his eyes at me, as though he sees right through to my thoughts. "I'm Bardhyl."

My gaze automatically swings to his powerful bicep, at the way the fabric pulls tautly over his strong chest at the slightest movement. My heart flutters at the sight.

I mentally shake my head—except my wolf is in my chest, pushing to get closer. Just what I need! She acts all coy and lusty while still living inside me, but what will she be like when she comes out?

The more I look at this shifter, the more I notice how handsome he is. My body screams out for him. My eyes do as well. So does my wolf. But he's just another minion to the Alpha.

I search the depth of his eyes for sympathy. When he pulls me by the hand toward the houses, I bite my cheek, reining in my anger.

"Where are you taking me?" I try to use my sweetest voice, hoping he'll find it in his heart to release me.

The smile he offers me melts me on the spot. His eyes seem to glint in the sunlight. With a strong nose and jawline, he is captivating. But he says nothing.

By the time we reach the courtyard with houses on either side of us, the sun is heavy on our backs. Around us, shifters are chatting, walking about, doing whatever it is they do. But panic is squeezing the hell out of my heart.

I trip over an uneven stone, and he catches my arm. "Please tell me where you're taking me. I want to return to my home. My parents will be looking for me."

He pauses before me, all strength and heat—dangerous. Arching a brow, he leans in close again, leaving me completely breathless. I shouldn't let his nearness get to me, but the image of him all over me is turning me on. "I adore the way you try to lie to me."

His grip doesn't let up, and suddenly we're flying across the cobblestones.

"Lie?" I huff, fighting to tear my hand from his iron grip. There's almost something intimate in the way he looks at me, as if he might sweep me up off my feet and carry me into the woods. I swallow, not completely averse to the idea…Wait! What am I thinking? Of course, I don't want that.

He turns and wrenches me across the open courtyard. I stumble behind him as we swing left between two homes, then turn left and then right, small stone houses all around us. Voices and cries of children come from inside the homes, as well as the succulent aromas of food cooking.

In seconds, he has my back pressed to the front door of a smaller home, his body trapping me. "I'm a fair man, and I owe you a kiss back." He smiles like a deviant before kissing me softly, teasing me.

I should push him back, or drive my knee into his groin. Instead, I'm losing myself to his affection, and he makes me forget all other thoughts.

My hands desperately clutch his tee, and I heave myself up on tippy-toes, taking his tongue in my mouth. Heavens, he feels incredible, tastes so delicious and masculine. My head screams this is wrong, to push this stranger away, but my wolf is pushing my body to taste him.

I groan against him as my whole body tenses. His lips drag over my cheek and to my neck just below my earlobe. His tongue flicks out against the tender flesh. I shiver beneath him. Dirty images fill my mind of what his mouth would feel like all over my body.

"I hate that I have to stop," he whispers.

The door behind me suddenly opens, and I'm falling backward into a dark room. I cry out, reaching for him, but I land on my ass as he stands in the doorway, grinning down at me. He grabs the door and shuts it, then he's gone.

"What the fuck?!"

It isn't long before the faint scent of floral perfume tickles my nose.

I freeze.

I'm not alone here.

CHAPTER 10

DUŠAN

Meira is a half-breed. Fuck! There's no way I can send her to Ander now, so trying to keep my word has been a damn waste of time. He won't accept her...not many will. She's a liability if her wolf does decide to come out. It will rip out of her body, killing her, but the beast that remains will be a savage brute that will kill everyone in sight.

This is why other packs kill half-breeds who haven't transformed once they hit puberty.

My wolf rumbles in my chest, shoving, pining for Meira. And I didn't want to see the truth smacking me in the face, didn't want to admit that fate had finally paid me a visit.

Her wolf has connected with mine. The

precursor for mating for life. Now I feel the need in my bones, in the way my wolf hums in her presence, at how my body awakens at the mere thought of her. Back in the bathroom, I barely held it together to stop myself from claiming her. I'd hoped it was nothing more than lust because the growing desire inside me will soon make her insatiable to me. But she poses a grave danger to my pack. I'll have to make sure she is always with an Alpha when not closed off in her room.

I scrub a hand down my face. How is this going to work, anyway? An Alpha with a weak half-breed, who's a time-bomb waiting to go off? I promised my pack safety. So why did the fates bring me together with Meira this way?

I pace up and down my office, fury burning through me.

"You will never amount to anything. No one will mate with you."

Father's words flare over my mind. With them comes rage, and I clench my fists. I promised myself I would make a difference to my pack, not become their burden like my father did to his.

Memories roll right over me, giving me no chance to shove them aside.

. . .

"*Don't,*" *I yell, lunging at my father who raises another hand to my mother. She's on the floor, bleeding and bruised, gasping for air. Her eyes turn to me as she mouths, 'run.'*

The thought of her suffering excited him. I see it in his dark eyes. "I warned you."

I threw myself into my monster of a father, a burly shifter, but still even my thin ten-year old body shoved him into a sideways stumble. Fury takes me, and I drive everything I have into him—punches, kicks, teeth. My fury simmers to a boiling point.

He shoves a hand behind me, snatches me by the scruff and hurls me across the room like I weigh nothing. I slam into the wall and slide down, my lungs gasping for air. I wipe away the useless tears...

"This is your fault," he growls, glaring at my mother. "You made him weak and useless."

His hand raises again, curled into a fist as he leans over my mother.

"Don't touch her," I scream, scrambling to my feet, but it's too late.

Everything is too late.

My world dies in that moment, ripped out from under me, and I know nothing will ever be the same.

The punches begin again and don't stop. The dull whacks soon turn to moist thuds.

The room tilts under me. My stomach lurches, and I run out of the room as I hurl out everything in my stomach.

*E*ven today I feel the hollowness inside me, my muscles so tense they might snap. My throat thickens at the memory I've tried so hard to bury away. To push away the images of the blood seeping over the cobblestone floor. That isn't how I want to remember my mother, crumpled and bleeding on the floor. I want to remember her as the caring woman who loved me, who hid me, who protected me.

As broken as Meira is, as unpredictable as her wolf is, I can't push her away.

Whether she accepts it or not, she's in trouble, and I will help her.

I try to clear my head and make sense of what to do next. To push away the feeling of emptiness.

This is why I stepped up to the role of Alpha. Shifters now turn to me when they have a problem, when they need help.

A howl comes from somewhere in the woods outside. The wolf run is on tonight—at the full moon, when we are all at our wildest. When even my rules won't tame the wolves in my pack. This is a night of recklessness, of releasing and being one with our true nature.

And it's the perfect time to see how much her wolf controls her.

I can't stop seeing the blood in the trashcan from her sickness. So much of it, and any human with this illness wouldn't have many days left. I suspect her wolf side has kept her alive, but for how much longer?

Bardhyl appears at my office door, and I clear my throat, raising my head. "Everything went well?" I ask.

He nods. "You're right. The girl is feisty."

There's a fire in my Fourth's eyes when he speaks of Meira. She has this impact on those she encounters.

"Yeah. Try dragging her through the woods to our settlement like I did." I shake my head as he laughs. "Anyway, we now need a replacement for her to send to the X-Clan Alpha. Tomorrow at first light, take a small group of hunters out in the woods and find another girl." All the girls we had on hand either found their mate amid Ash Wolves, or went to another pack in Europe.

"Of course." He pauses for a moment, looking ready to ask me something.

"What is it?"

"What will you do with Meira?" Concern weaves through his words. His eyes hood as he breathes heavily.

"I'll find a way to save her. Otherwise, she can't stay here." Fear knots in my gut. I look down and stare at the comm video screen, knowing I have to contact Ander for an update, but I feel physically ill at the idea of parting from Meira. The world was meant to fall into place when I met my mate... Except it's just been a clusterfuck of a mess ever since I found her.

"You said she threw up a lot of blood, right?" Bardhyl asks. "That means the sicker she gets, the weaker she becomes. She'll be unable to stop the beast from finally breaking out."

Of course he's fucking right. "So we don't have much time. Tonight's the full moon. That's when I need to start."

Bardhyl nods. With a bow of his head, he leaves

the office. He's a lot quieter tonight than usual, but I shake that off.

I'm left alone, and I can't stop thinking about Meira. How she affected me from the beginning, how there are so many things I want to do to her. My wolf demands I claim her before it's too late, but it's not that simple now. Panic fills me at the thought that I'll lose her before I get that chance, and that quickly turns to anger at her being a half-breed.

I've had my share of women. Enough of them that I don't remember how many. They eagerly take to my bed, and I fill them over and over. But I've never found the high I'm searching for, that feeling that ignites my fire and draws me to them, that awakens my wolf.

This hellcat is just that, and my whole body shudders in her presence. I can still smell her sugary scent from the baths, the slick that tightens my balls. I feel it in my veins, from the top of my head to my toes to the tip of my cock.

I know I'm not the only one whom Meira's allure has called to her side.

Meira

"Come close. Don't be afraid," a female's voice calls me from within the dark room.

I stiffen, blinking as my eyes adjust to the darkness. "Who are you?"

A flicker of candlelight erupts from the end of the room, revealing a woman in her mid-forties sitting in a rocking chair, her lap covered in blankets, her eyes shadowy and exhausted.

"I'm Kinley. Come join me." She nods to the wooden chair across from her. Nearby on the table is a collection of books, a pot of tea, and a single cup. She's been snoozing by the look of sleep still clinging to her eyes.

"I'm sorry," I say, retreating to the door. "I think there's been a mistake. I'll let you sleep." My hand reaches for the door handle to try to leave, but it's locked.

"Meira, this is no mistake."

I stand still and glance across the small living room. A curtain covers the windows, the fireplace is unlit, and this home has simple furnishings. The room smells stuffy.

"You live with death, girl," she murmurs. "You

wish you were born differently. You believe that if you can just keep the wolf away, everything would be fine, don't you?"

"What do you know about it?" I whisper softly, almost unsure if I want to hear the answer.

She glances to the empty chair across from her, and I reluctantly cross the room, then take a seat.

"I know that if you keep ignoring the inevitable, it will be too late to save yourself."

Something tightens in my solar plexus, as she's way too close to the truth for comfort. My whole life, I've lived with the fear that my wolf hasn't shown, and that when it does, I'll lose all control. I accepted long ago that I am better off without her.

"It's worked this long," I answer.

"And what is your plan for the future? Keep running? A wolf won't stay at bay forever."

I study this woman with short sandy hair, wearing a white button-up shirt with frills around the collar. She's pretty and speaks with a kind voice, but frustration fills me with her vagueness.

"Kinley, I'm not sure what you want me to say or do. Or why I'm here in the first place. I don't even know you."

Her gray eyes glint in the candlelight. "My mother was a human, and she died when she gave birth to me. My father was killed and turned into an infected on my fifteenth birthday. My whole life has been survival, just like the lives of each one of the Ash Wolves outside. Just like you. And I'll be honest, Dušan asked me to talk to you."

Her admittance has a jagged edge to it, like she doesn't feel comfortable with it, either.

"Thank you for sharing."

"Go collect yourself a cup from the kitchen." She points her chin to the other side of the room. There's a plate with freshly baked flatbread and venison. "Bring that over too. You look starved."

Kinley speaks gently, and there's something almost comforting about her. She reminds me of my mother, and there's a warmth spreading over my chest. I'm on my feet and across the dark room, returning with the items in no time.

She pours me tea and the waft of citrus finds my nose. I collect one of the flatbreads, which is the size of my hand, and tear off pieces before popping them into my mouth. Hunger has me salivating, and I eat three in record time.

Kinley watches me as she sips her tea. "My neighbor makes them for me. She's ninety years old and still incredible in the kitchen."

Washing down the food with citrus tea, I set it back on the table. "Tell me about Dušan?"

"His father was a ruthless leader, but after his death, Dušan took over and changed everything in his pack. *Everything*—including the pack rules and moving us all to this settlement, but especially when it comes to protecting females. He will kill anyone who harms a female." There's a knowingness in her expression, as if she's experienced that first hand.

"Why?"

"The old Alpha was violent, especially to his mate and children." She glances away for a moment, then clears her throat. I see the sorrow on her face. "But there's nowhere else I'd rather live now. Not after what happened to me." She lowers her hand and peels away the layers of blankets over her lap.

My gaze follows the movement, and underneath, she's wearing gray trousers. They sit loosely over thin legs. They're so bony, something tightens in my stomach.

I want to look away, but I can't. The top half of her body seems normal, but it looks like she's shriveled on the lower half.

"I'm paralyzed from the waist down," she says.

"Happened when I was twenty years old and underwent my first transformation."

I blink at her words. "You survived?"

"Yes." Her eyes light up.

I'm completely stunned by her reveal.

"So even now, can you transform into your wolf?"

She smiles widely. "Of course. My legs will never work again in either form, but I'm alive."

My throat closes. I shift in my seat, unease curling over my spine. Just looking at her breaks my heart.

Is this my fate? I don't want to spend the rest of my life closed up in a house. I've always been on the run and lived in the wilderness. Being alone and unable to walk or run would kill me.

"I know what you're thinking," she murmurs. "But my transformation came when a rogue wolf attacked me. It was my fated mate's wolf energy, a wolf from the Shadowlands Sector, that saved me from dying when my beast broke out of me that day. The rogue wolf severed my nerves and put me here."

My hands shake by my side. "But I've heard of no half-breeds who've survived if they transform after puberty."

"I am living proof that it's possible, if you just believe."

My mouth dries as her words soothe my wolf, and for the first time in my life, I feel like maybe there is hope for me after all.

CHAPTER 11

MEIRA

"Please don't lock me in there," I plead with Bardhyl, who shoves open the door to a seemingly random room in the castle. Once Kinley's mate returned home, Bardhyl collected me from her home and brought me back to the castle without so much as a word.

"Don't make me carry you inside. It's for your own safety."

There's an edge to his voice, which scares me. I step into the empty room. No furniture, just a lit fireplace.

He shuts the door and locks me in.

I dig my hand into my pocket and pull out the two metal rods from the last room, then make my way to the door. This palace has old locks which are ridiculously easy to pick. I wait a little while to ensure Bardhyl is gone.

I spent hours with Kinley, listening to her stories about living alone before her transformation. The similarities between our stories are uncanny. By the end, I decided I really liked her. But I also don't want to be closed up in a room and wait for Dušan to come and just mark me. I've met three Alphas who have connected with my wolf, and I want to understand that more.

Kinley suggested I spend more time getting to know my potential mates, as the transition will be easier. And tonight, I want to visit Lucien and talk to him to see if there's any way I can avoid a mating with Dušan. I hate him for kidnapping me, and I hate him more because of the way my wolf and body betray me around him. How they long for him. If I had my head on straight, I wouldn't dream about kissing him. It's best we stay apart. Lucien seems the most approachable of the Alphas I've met so far.

I jam the two metal rods into the keyhole and twist and fiddle with them until I hear the familiar clicking sound.

Quickly, I slip out of the room and speed down the corridor. The moon is full tonight. I can feel it on my skin, and the wolf inside me stirs more than usual.

A wolf bays in the distance.

Not stopping, I move in and out of hallways, up steps, and then repeat. It's only when I'm standing in a narrow arched door looking out into the woods behind the fortress that I quickly forget about Lucien. I've found a way out of the castle, and maybe while the night cloaks the ground, I can find a possible way through the surrounding fence.

I still haven't come to terms with the idea of an Alpha marking and owning me.

So I slip outside into the balmy night. Overhead, the enormous moon hangs low, illuminating the mountains in its silvery hue.

With quick steps, I head away from the main part of the fortress and rush into the forest inside the fence.

Twigs crunch, and I twist around to find no one there. I keep going as more and more growls and snapping of foliage move in closer. I pause and press my back to a tree, my heart galloping. Shadows dart around me. Maybe this is a mistake... I should come out first thing in the morning to find a way out.

A figure lingers near—out of sight, but whoever it is, they aren't leaving me.

I scan the trees behind me for escape.

There's no answer, but danger snaps in the dark across my skin. Still, I know the man is still there. I can now smell him, his scent...his desire. My boots scrape the soft forest floor as I step back once more. A howl cuts through the air in the distance. It's low and sorrowful, and the sound slices through me like a knife.

A desperate howl sounds...One call of a beast to another.

That's what is inside me—a beast that refuses to come out. I swallow the bitter tang of acid as a snap of a twig comes from somewhere to my right.

Shadows shift. I feel them more than see them, just like I feel everything around me now.

Like the moon...

The silver glow throbs in the air, sending shudders along my skin. My heart pounds in response, the tremors carving through my body.

Another sound cuts through the air, only this is somewhere behind me.

"They're coming for you."

I flinch at the words and jerk my gaze to the darkened thatch of trees. Dušan steps out of the shadows, striding with long, purposeful steps until he stands in the moonlight.

His soft blue eyes look almost silver in the night. I'm trapped in them, nailed to the spot as he steps closer. His long, dark hair dances in the air with the movement and my breath catches in my chest.

"I told you," I whisper, my voice hoarse. "I want nothing to do with any of this."

"And still, that won't stop them. Why did you leave your room?" He gravitates toward me in slow motion. My earlier fear fizzles in comparison to the delirious arousal burning through me for this Alpha.

That's how it is with us. Push. Pull. Gravitating one minute, and repelled in the next. Thoughts crowd my mind, panicked thoughts filled with the image of us.

"Other wolves, they'll keep coming and coming after you tonight. They won't know how not to. One way or another, your wolf has to come out. You have to be marked, Meira. For your own safety. Now that they have your scent."

"And your desire, right?" My response comes out as a whisper.

There's a twitch at the corner of his eye, a nerve

flaring in response. He lowers his attention, taking in my body as I reach out and step backward.

"I'd be lying if I said I wasn't at least a little intrigued," he says.

Intrigued? A hard bark of laughter tears along my throat. "Nice choice of words. Only what's to say you aren't exactly like them?" I jerk my head toward the piercing call that dances on the wind.

My body thrums with power, like paws smacking the ground. Tonight, the wild wolves are set loose, just like Dušan said… and they're coming for me. Their hunger. Their need. Heat mingles with terror, and it's a dangerous cocktail.

"*I* don't know that you aren't." My voice trembles, needing and desperate. "I don't know that at all. I don't know you, don't know any of this."

Run. The need roars inside me. Take a chance on my own. I'm fast and lithe, able to scurry along the rocks and climb the mountain faster than someone like the bulky Alpha in front of me.

If I can escape the settlement tonight, I can find a crevice in the surrounding mountains and slip in. I'll wait until morning, wait until they finally give up the hunt…I can make my way back home.

Home.

The word resounds. Where is my home?

Dušan jerks his gaze to the right, his lips curling, a savage snarl spilling from his mouth. "Decide, Meira, and decide fast. They're coming."

Panic tears through me as a growl cuts through the trees. Dušan lifts his hands as long, black claws punch out from the tips. He turns his head and takes one look at me standing there petrified as another blur races toward us, cutting between the trees.

There's a moment that passes between us, one filled with desperation and duty before he rips his attention from mine and mutters, "Fuck."

He lunges away, lowering his head as he charges into the gloom of the forest. The heavy thump of his steps beats a panicked drum inside my head. Branches snap, mingling with a guttural roar.

A brutal thud comes moments later. Savage, primal growls fill the night. My stomach clenches with the sound as a howl comes tearing through the bushes in front of me.

I have no choice. I do the only thing I can—turn and run.

My throat tightens as a terrifying howl comes from the direction Dušan has disappeared. Is that him? The thunder in my head grows louder, crashing like a crescendo as images come to life. Dušan hurt, lying there bleeding and broken, all because he wants me for himself.

I shake my head as tears blur my view. I scan the tree line, finding a trail that carves a clear path to the part of the mountain within the metal walls. My knees tremble, locking as I stumble forward. I pray my legs will hold, and hurry, leaving the Alpha and the pack behind.

Guilt swallows me. I find myself slowing as I hit the bushes and turning back around. The unmerciful sounds are sickening. Fists and claws flay flesh until a piercing, shattering cry fills the night...and what follows is silence.

Empty silence.

Warmth slips down my cheeks as I look back to the trees. I'm on my own now, on my own with desperation and what little courage I have left.

Dušan's pale blue eyes haunt me as I stagger forward, my boots finding the worn path amongst the trees. A couple of other wolves come for me, swarming the forest all around me. Their male scent so pungent, it's like a rag down my throat. They smell so familiar.

I drive my boots against the ground and run as

fast as I can. Nails pierce the flesh of my palm. Something emerges out of the infernal darkness.

"Where do you think you're going, female?"

The warning plunges like ice through my veins. His long, blond hair shines as he moves closer. I haven't seen him before, and I don't find him handsome in the slightest. I skid to a stop, my heart pounding so loud, I can barely think.

"Leave me alone," I warn, my voice cracking and trembling.

"I can't do that." He sucks in hard breaths and glides near, just like Dušan did.

But unlike the towering midnight-haired Alpha, this one keeps coming, lengthening his long strides. White fangs glow in the dark. "Now, I can tell you I'll be gentle." He jerks his attention toward the trees. "But the rest will be here before we know it...and I need to have my fill of you."

I shake my head as a tremor slices through me.

"God, I love the scent of your fear," the male growls, his voice savage and unkind. "Don't worry. You'll be wearing my mark before long."

He reaches up and grasps the front of his shirt. With one brutal yank, the fabric splits, tearing from his chest before he drops the ruined garment to the ground.

Muscles ripple in the night. All that power, all that lust. His dark eyes glitter like steel in the night. Panic floods me, clamping my insides tight.

"No," I whisper. "*Please*. No."

He's on me in an instant, lunging to close the distance in a panicked heartbeat. One hand goes around my arm, the other closes over my breast. He looks down at me. "I'll be gentle, *next time*, I promise."

Claws pierce the fabric of my dress. The sound of tearing cloth starts before a low and unmistakable warning growl comes from behind me. "Take your fucking hands off her."

I stiffen at the sound. Hope surges in my chest as a whimper slips from my lips. Dušan approaches, and the smell of blood and power washes over me. "I won't ask you again, Vin."

"She's not marked." The male turns to pierce me with his dangerous stare. "Not yet."

The sting from his claws cuts deeper, pressing in around my breasts. Is this what it means to be marked? Am I now this savage male's property? Terror drives in deep. "Please, no. Not you. Not like this."

Vin wrenches his gaze to mine as he curls his lips. "You don't want me, female?"

"No, she doesn't," Dušan answers for me. "Now remove your claws before I remove them for you… with your own fucking teeth."

There's a wince as fear drives to the surface of the wolf's eyes. Dušan smells savage, the thick, cloying metallic scent of blood hanging heavy in the air.

It isn't his blood.

Not his.

Relief courses through me as Vin unfurls his fingers and lowers his hand.

"Now let her go."

A low, pissed-off sound flies from the male's lips before he lets me go.

"Meira," Dušan murmurs.

A connection between us surges.

"Hurry," he whispers. "Run farther up the mountain inside the settlement, and I'll find you."

That bond between us throbs with life. Something crashes through the bushes behind us. I swallow hard, give a nod and step sideways, whipping my gaze from his in the last moment before I lash forward.

I race into the night, bounding over fallen logs and around thick, thorny brambles. Thorns snag on my dress, scratching deep. I push down the sting and keep on running, clambering blindly, pushing myself forward with the knowledge that the edge of the metal fence should be near.

The mountain towers above, a monolithic giant brooding and dangerous. I suck in sawing breaths and glance over my shoulder.

I can't hear them anymore. I can't feel Dušan.

My hands tremble as I climb farther, focusing on the motion of lifting my foot on the steep ground and pushing my body higher and higher, until I have to stop to catch my breath. I clutch a hold of the rock and lower my head to the surface.

Trees spread out like a blanket far below me. I'm high up...*really* high.

"Take your fucking hand off her." Dušan's words fill my head as I straighten and set my gaze to the task.

He hurt and maimed others for me.

All to save me.

Still, instinct leads the way. I move slower now, pulling myself up onto a small dirt ledge on the side of the mountain overlooking the fortress below. I just drop to my knees there, panting.

Silence finds me, clutching ahold of the edge. I barely hang on.

Down there. Down there, Dušan is battling one, two…ten of them to protect me.

I shudder. *"Hide. I'll find you."*

I hold on to those words, looking around. The soft glow of the full moon hugs the contours of the mountain. I can't climb anymore. I get to my feet and stagger backward from the edge, shoving my heels against the stone until my spine meets the coolness of the mountain.

Lightning flickers high up in the clouds, far off in the distance. Up here, the world spreads out before me, leaving only thoughts and memories behind. I drag my knees upward and pull them close.

Is Dušan still fighting? How many can he battle before one of them takes him down? I bite my lower lip as a shudder courses through my body. A snarl echoes through my mind, savage and unwelcome.

"No, stay away from me," I whisper, stilling the beast inside me that pushes forward.

Claws scrape under the skin of my knees before the tips push against my skin.

Fear bursts through me that my wolf will come now—tonight. *Here.*

I close my eyes as the faint echo of thunder

rumbles through the sky, and that creature inside me reacts, lifting her head to inhale the faint scent of ozone.

I don't know how long I wait. Minutes feel like a lifetime as I watch the storm slowly creep closer, lightening the sky with neon flashes of white. As each second rolls it toward me, I feel that desperation inside.

I need to leave this place—leave Dušan—or by morning, there'll be no reason to leave. By morning, they'll have found me. Tears slip down my cheeks at the guilt I feel for sneaking out. I brush them away with the back of my hand and then shove against the ground.

"Don't tell me you're leaving already."

The low, guttural growl is punctured with slow heavy breaths. Dušan limps forward, coming out of the darkness like a god. Lightning cleaves through the sky behind him, and for a second, my heart pounds into the back of my throat.

He stumbles forward, holding his left arm against his body. He tries to hide the pain from me as he lifts his gaze, but wolves heal fast. A long scratch mars his cheek and his shirt is torn along the middle. One shoulder completely gone, torn by fangs and claws.

His boot scrapes as he stumbles forward, his ocean blue eyes searching my face before he slowly takes in all of me.

He saved me, protected me, and he could have died in the process.

"Why?" The word slips from my lips. "Why risk your life like that?"

"If I have to explain it, then I've done a pretty piss poor job of showing you before now."

My breath catches as he approaches me. Only this time, I'm not moving backward. This time, I'm not running.

"I don't want this." I shake my head. "I don't want any of this."

"And yet, that won't change a thing. You have a wolf inside you, Meira. One you can't cut out. One you can't deny forever. You're at the crossroads here. You can either die, or embrace what you are and learn that with the downsides, there are some pretty amazing positives."

"Yeah, like what?"

He reaches up, grasps the back of his shirt, and drags it over his head. Muscles cord, clenching tightly as he drops the ruined garment to the ground. "Faster healing abilities, for one thing." His arm doesn't droop as much anymore, and I catch him straightening. "And also smell," he continues. "For instance, I can smell the hares running frantically from the storm…can you?"

I draw in the air through my nose, letting the sweet scent carry me away. Panic tastes bitter under the sweetness. "Yes."

"Just like how I can smell your wolf. I can smell her hunger—her need. I can smell that she's ready to come through. That she *wants* to come through."

My pulse speeds up with his words. The thought of that—of being out of control—terrifies me. "I…"

"I can't fight them forever," he murmurs as he steps closer. "But I will for as long as I can, if that's what you want."

"Will it hurt?" I search for the truth. "I don't want to die."

"Not the way I want to do it." He lifts his hand. "And we don't have to…We don't have to have sex, if that's what you want."

"But you'll still mark me, won't you?"

Sadness flares for a second in his eyes. "Yes. My mark will show my claim. No other male will touch you. Not unless you want them to."

"Unless I want them to?"

"Don't worry." He swallows hard. "I won't force you into my bed, Meira."

My throat tightens. The thought of being in his bed fills me, just like the lightning floats in the sky over the valley. Do I want that? Do I want to belong to him that way?

My heart clenches tightly, answering for me. "What do I have to do?"

His eyes widen for a second before he steps near. I flinch as he lifts his hand. The movement is automatic. Still, that doesn't stop him from wincing. "Turn around and sit."

Turn around and sit? I don't know what I expected, but it wasn't that. "Can't you just bite my hand?"

A sad smile crests his lips. There's a slow shake of his head. "It doesn't work like that, unfortunately."

"Then how does it work?"

"Turn around, Meira. I promise, your wolf will lead the way."

I stare into his eyes, finding nothing but compassion and desire, and finally putting my trust in him, I turn around to give him my back. I sink to the ground, crossing my legs. I gasp as he moves. I become aware of him...intently aware of the close proximity of his body to mine. The way he towers over me and then drops to the ground.

I remember Kinley's story, how her mate helped her wolf cross. Maybe this is what I need. Help to release my wolf and no longer be an outcast.

"Hands on the ground in front," he orders.

My heart lunges. Still, I do as he instructs.

His fingers brush the hair from the back of my neck before he leans close. Warm lips meet my flesh. I close my eyes with the contact and try to remember to breathe.

Thunder growls overhead as he presses his chest against my back. He pushes against me, making me lean forward until my hands take my weight. I rise up on my knees as he hunkers down above.

He is so gentle, so incredibly gentle and yet there is nothing soft about him. He's all power, all Alpha. The heat of his body melts into my spine, easing that constant ache in my body. His lips trail down, sliding over my shirt to press on my back.

"Mother have mercy," he growls, his voice husky.

My wolf moves closer. The sound of her soft, padding steps in my mind mingles with the heat of his body. A snarl slips from my lips, rumbling in the center of my chest before I realize it's there.

"That's it," he whispers. "Come to me."

I hunker down against the warmth of the stone. Heat radiates from within me, pooling between my thighs and spilling outward. Electricity dances across my breasts, making my nipples tighten as Dušan kisses the place beneath my ear.

"You ready, Meira?" he murmurs against my ear.

I don't register a word, don't realize a thing as he grinds his hips against the curve of my ass. Fangs graze that soft flesh behind my ear, unleashing a surge of arousal. I moan and drop my lower body to the ground.

Dušan follows me, bracing most of his body with his shoulders as he pins me down. There's a slow nip, playful and teasing. I curl my fingers as my wolf pushes closer. Raindrops smack the mountain with a hiss. The sky is alive, blazing neon white, and in the electric glow, my wolf lunges, driving herself higher.

With an unmerciful growl, Dušan bites down, sinking his fangs into the back of my neck. The orgasm comes out of nowhere, barreling on top of me as I grind my body against the stone. Pain slashes my palms, but the sting is gone in an instant as I feel my body shift.

Desire swallows the roar inside my head. Still, Dušan holds on, not letting me go. A shiver races along my arms until warmth moves in.

Dušan bites harder. There's no pain, no terror, just arousal, and as the neon glow of lightning dulls, he releases me…and pulls backward.

I lie there, his heavy breath on my neck, my wolf on the edge… so close.

"Something is wrong," he whispers into the moment that is perfect in every way. Except it isn't perfect, is it?

"She feels stuck," I say.

I feel his weight lift from my back. Strong hands clasp my waist and draw me to my knees. Arms wrap around my waist, his solid chest flush to my back.

Shadows move down below, flitting amid the trees.

His words are in my ear. "It's okay. It might take a bit more of a nudge."

I hear the smirk in his voice, and I know what he's implying. Heat surges through me at the thought of him taking me.

"Yes." I gasp the word.

His hold tightens in response, his breaths fast and shallow. "Not tonight. I won't rush this."

We stay like that for a long moment, and I melt against him. "You've marked me as yours, haven't you?"

He doesn't respond right away, instead sweeping the hair away from my neck. Warm lips find my ear. "Partially. Tomorrow, we will finish. But you are now mine. Everyone will know that now and leave you alone."

Mine. That is all I hear.

CHAPTER 12

MEIRA

"Are you ready?" Lucien asks from the doorway to Dušan's bedroom. Leaning a shoulder against the doorframe, his hands folded over his chest, he studies me with a strange expression. Hooded eyes, curved lips, and a mysterious glint in his stunning, gray irises. "It's a gorgeous morning, and Dušan asked me to take you to breakfast. He's got a few things to get done today."

For those few moments, I let myself drown in this perfect image of this specimen of a shifter. His biceps flex as he drops his arms by his side, then runs a hand through his short, brown hair. He is a wall of muscle. Captivating. Dangerous…because he puts dirty thoughts in my mind. My cheeks heat at the very possibility that somehow my wolf wants more than one man.

He's wearing dark jeans hanging low on his hips, a wrinkled blue t-shirt, and brown cowboy boots. Which intrigues me.

"What's with the boots?" I clear my throat and walk around the bed to collect the new lace-up sandals Dušan brought me last night. I'm wearing a sky-blue dress that falls to mid-thigh. The fabric is the softest material I've ever touched. He even arranged for black lace underwear and a bra. He then kept his word and let me sleep alone in his bed, which I appreciated.

"They're comfortable to wear," he answers, but I can tell he's lying.

I straighten and run my hands down the fabric. I can't get the previous night out of my mind, and instinctively, I reach up to the back of my neck where he bit me. Where he left his mark. The skin is rough from his teeth marks, and just remembering the moment sends a shiver of excitement down my spine. I never expected the Alpha to be so gentle, to bring me to arousal with such tenderness. The night was a whirlwind of being swept into a perfect memory of fear and seduction.

Turning around, I find Lucien studying me, like

he can read my thoughts. I try to swallow the lump in my throat, but it feels impossible. I'm torn between hating these shifters and desiring them. I loathe myself for it, but I can't seem to back away, either.

"Have you heard of the saying, *'wrong place, wrong time,'* gorgeous?" he asks.

"Yeah."

"I know you feel like a string of bad luck and bad decisions brought you to our doorstep, but do you ever think fate has a funny way of forcing things that are meant to be?"

"So you place your trust in fate?" I walk around the bed and note his gaze trailing down my body, all the way down to my gold sandals.

I know I shouldn't feel the things I do, but near Lucien, my breath catches in my throat and heat flares over my skin. He looks at me like he'll rip the dress off me and pin me to the wall as he fucks me. Fire curls up and over my neck at the image now smothering my thoughts.

"There are some things that are too strange, too powerful to be pure coincidences, don't you think?" he asks.

I lick my dry lips and nod as we both leave my bedroom and walk past the guard at my door.

Maybe being so close to Lucien isn't such a great idea. Farther down the hall, we turn left toward a set of circular stairs heading upstairs. "Is that what you were brought up believing?" I reply. "My childhood was mostly about running and finding a new safe home. I didn't even know what fate was for the longest time."

He looks over at me with a soft look, brimming with sympathy.

"Don't do that," I say, my cheeks heating with shame. "I don't want your pity."

"That's not pity, Meira. It's understanding. We all have different stories, and I'm not saying one is better than the other. But some of us have had a shitty start in this infected world, even more so than others."

I open my mouth to speak, but I forget my words when we step out onto a small balcony jutting out from the base of the pointed tower roof. A gust of cool air hits me and swirls around me. My mouth drops open at the small table and chairs set up with plates of food, but my attention devours the sight from up here. I move toward the metal railing encircling the open area and stare out over the most spectacular view of the wild Carpathian Mountains surrounding us.

"Beautiful, isn't it?" Lucien stands behind me. I feel his presence so close to me. My skin ripples with goose bumps in anticipation—with the need to have him touch me and press himself against me. I shudder.

"It's spectacular." I glance down below to the woods just outside the metal walls of the settlement. Small movements down there catch my attention, and I squint for a better look since we're so high.

"Do you see that?" I point down.

Lucien steps beside me to look down, our arms grazing. His skin is fiery hot, and I resist the urge to lean in closer to him. He distracts me so easily.

You need to stop, I scold myself, knowing that I am in enough trouble after last night, and I need to rein in my desires.

The wind blows through my hair as we both stare into the woods, where half a dozen undead lurch closer to the fence. Two of them drop to their knees, hunched forward as if feeding. The others soon join them.

"Do you think it's a dead animal?" I ask, remembering that I saw undead emerging from the nearby woods when I first arrived. They've definitely fed here before, so they'll never leave if they keep finding food so close to the settlement.

Lucien doesn't respond for a moment but nods. "Yeah, maybe." There's a tightness in his voice.

I turn to face him, my back to the railing, and he straightens, standing so tall and so close to me that I can't think. My chest tightens at the dirty thoughts that play with my mind.

I dip my gaze to his full lips and my body trembles, then to the scar along his collarbone. This is a barbaric world when fighting is the only way to survive.

"Your heart is beating so fast. Are you afraid of me?" he murmurs.

"No, not afraid of you." I'm scared of the lack of control I have around him, at the arousal that leads me to draw my lower lip into my mouth.

The small growl that comes from him tells me I'm playing a dangerous game. He moves closer, and I don't draw away.

I lean forward with closed eyes until our lips press together. I can't think for those few seconds when the world seems to hold us prisoner in this perfect moment. In a moment where I'm kissing the shifter under Dušan's command, the Alpha who marked me as his last night.

He parts his mouth, and I do the same, our tongues mingling. Sparks flutter down my spine and fire melts between my thighs, coating my underwear in seconds. He isn't pulling back, and I'm not stopping. I don't want to end this, so I place my hands on his biceps as he wraps me in his arms. I press my breasts against his chest, my nipples rubbing over his muscular pecs.

I love the groaning sounds he makes.

Our breaths are racing, his kiss deep and dominating as he explores my mouth with his tongue—licking me, owning me.

He breaks away first, and I open my eyes to find doubt in his eyes. A chill settles in my bones.

"Even if I can't stop thinking of you, we shouldn't do this." The ache in his steel-gray eyes tightens my throat, and embarrassment crashes into me. It shouldn't, but an uncomfortable burning climbs over me.

"Why?" I ask.

"Because we'll both get hurt. I should never have kissed you." He looks away and turns abruptly toward the table. "We better eat before the wind carries away our meal."

I move toward the round table that's bolted to the stone ground, including the chairs. The metal is cold against the back of my legs when I sit down. The ache in my chest deepens, and I turn my attention to the food. There's a plate filled with cooked strips of meat, jam pastries, and even a round loaf of sliced bread with dripping butter.

"Lucien, we didn't do anything wrong." I surprise myself to find that I'm reaching out to him when I should be pushing these wolves away. My head hurts with confusion, with a need I can't comprehend.

"It doesn't matter," he says. "Eat up."

Did I hear him right? "Of course it matters."

He reaches over and fills his plate before eating.

"What do you mean?" I ask as he closes his eyes and makes a rumbling sound in his chest. When he looks at me again, there is sorrow in his eyes.

I don't know what to say. I'm getting myself in too deep, letting emotions carry me away. Lately, I've struggled to make sense of my body's reactions. My wolf may respond to these Alphas and yearn for them, but is she really that trustworthy? She's a beast inside me, refusing to emerge, and she could be the death of me.

Am I being foolish believing that what I'm feeling is anything but animalistic attraction?

We eat breakfast with small talk after that. He

isn't opening up about why he pulled away, and maybe it's none of my business. Maybe he is doing me a favor. Because clearly I can't seem to control my instincts around the three Alphas I've met in this pack. I've kissed all three and my wolf insists she wants them all. Something must definitely be broken inside of me.

Once we finish, he walks me to Dušan's bedroom.

"Meira," he says from the doorway. "I think it's better this way." Then he closes the door and leaves. And I'm left utterly confused and hurt.

Dušan

Night drapes the heavens as I'm marching back to my bedroom after the longest day. Fire simmers in my veins. I finally got a hold of Mad, who insisted he and Caspian were simply being hospitable and planned to return soon. He gave me nothing and hid everything that was really going on. I can discern it in his eyes, in his voice. The idiot even tried to joke about Ander losing grip of his pack, all over an Omega he hadn't yet completely claimed.

What Ander does with his pack isn't our business, and Mad needs to check the mess in his own backyard before throwing stones.

When he returns, I'll make him tell me everything or he's out. Bardhyl is right. Unless Mad pulls his shit together, he needs to go. As my Second, I need someone whom I can trust, and right now, I suspect he's doing something really stupid that's going to come back on me.

My footsteps strike the stone, reverberating in the hall. Stopping in front of my bedroom door, I draw in a sharp inhale to calm down. I don't want to scare Meira. All day, she's been on my mind, her scent in my nostrils, her taste on my tongue. Tonight, I will bring out her wolf—our energies will merge. Knowing the danger she poses to herself and the pack means I need to do this tonight. Last night, her wolf was ready to come out, eager for escape. And I'm about to give it a big nudge.

I unlock the door with the key in my pocket and walk inside.

Meira turns toward me, surprise widening her eyes, her hand holding a ceramic jug on which the bottom has fallen out. The pale yellow nightgown she wears is drenched, the cloth sticking to her body, curving over her perky breasts, following the tightness of her stomach. I almost choke on my breath as I take all of her in.

I stare at the dark hair at the apex of her thighs, at the delicious circles of her areolas pressed to the wet material.

Fuck!

"I think the jug had a crack in it," she says with a crooked smile.

I kick the door shut behind me and lock it. My cock punches against my pants, balls tightening. At first, all I can do is just stare at the wet nightgown, at her gorgeous body.

Pulling myself back to attention, I hurry forward to where she stands barefoot amid shards of ceramic. "Don't move."

I kneel and pick up the large pieces first, then I meticulously find all the small ones. I try to ease back my own hunger and remember a question I have been meaning to ask her. "Meira, out of curiosity how did you escape from the aircraft?"

"Mad and Caspian were too busy arguing about being late so when I was dragged on, Mad forgot to tie me up, then as soon as he went to the cockpit, I ran."

"Appreciate your honesty." I dump the pieces of ceramic into the trashcan and mentally shake my head at Mad's carelessness. Though it does seem odd since he's usually so meticulous with details.

Meira starts to walk across the room.

"Didn't I just say not to move?"

She stiffens at my order. I march closer and sweep her into my arms and then carry her to the bed before laying her onto her back.

"Did you step on any broken pieces?" I ask, sitting on the end of the bed, where I lift her feet up onto my lap.

I dust her soles clear, including her toes, and she squirms, giggling.

"You're tickling me."

"Hold still." I run my fingers gently over her feet, to hear more of her beautiful laughter. I inspect the skin for any cuts. She has such small, adorable feet. Slowly I massage her feet and toes, and I feel her relaxing.

"I really appreciate your help, but I'm not hurt." She squirms from my tickly touch.

When I turn to face her, she's leaning back on bent elbows, the material of the nightgown pulled taught over her chest, its transparency hiding nothing.

Goddamn, she's fucking beautiful. Her tiny curvy body calls to me.

"So, what's the plan for tonight?" she asks. "Dinner, then a stroll through the woods?" That dirty smile gives me a painful hard-on.

"There's only one thing I plan to do with you tempting me like that." I stand up from the bed and start unbuttoning my shirt, never lifting my gaze from her widening eyes.

She quickly glances down to her nightgown, then hastily lashes her hands over breasts. "Crap! You distracted me when you came in."

She rolls away from me, but I snatch her ankles and drag her down the bed toward me where I stand. The skirt of her nightgown rides up her legs, and a flash of dark hair between her thighs appears. She gasps and quickly shoves the fabric down over herself, but my cock throbs so damn hard now. All I can picture is spreading those gorgeous thighs and burying myself inside her.

Our mating heat rises through me, lifting the hairs on my arms. My balls grow heavy with the promise of this hellcat. With the way she looks at me, she feels that connection, the arousal, the growing need.

A gasp escapes past those gorgeous rosy lips.

I pull open my black shirt, noting her dipping gaze. Her cheeks redden, and I can't hold back the smile as I unclip the buttons on my sleeves. I slip the shirt off and lay it across the couch behind me.

"Dušan, I d-don't know... No, I... Shit!" She stumbles over her words and it's adorable that she thinks anything she says will change what's coming her way.

"We're completing the mating tonight, Meira. We have to bring your wolf out. You know this."

She's shaking her head, but her body betrays her as she pushes the skin-tight fabric of her nightgown between her legs. Her hand slyly rubs her heat. Her slick scent fills the air, and I've barely touched her. The magnetism between our wolves from the marking has connected us, and now it's calling to her, to me. It's intoxicating, dragging me deeper and deeper.

She gasps, and my cock aches, digging against my pants.

"Take it off," I order. "Show me how you touch yourself."

"No!" She pulls back, while watching me like

I'm the devil, but fighting against it will only bring her agonizing pain.

I reach out for her and snatch the thin fabric with two hands, tearing it in two with my bare hands. In one quick move, I rip it open all the way to her chest.

Those perfect breasts bounce, and I groan with unimaginable desire. She clenches her bent legs together, staring at me like a terrified deer.

"There are consequences if you don't obey, Meira. Now take it off."

"I… I shouldn't want you so badly, when all I want to do is shove you out that window."

A chuckle bursts past my throat, and it feels incredible to be laughing. "You can hate me, but tonight, we are bringing out your wolf. And you will beg for me."

"Never!" She spits the word at me, and I love her fierceness. It's exactly what I need by my side, someone who will hold her own, who will help lead my pack. She just needs to now grow physically strong.

I reach down and unbuckle my pants. "Take off the nightgown, Meira. I won't ask next time." I need her naked, need that luscious, curvy body to be all mine.

What we feel for each other is primal, our wolves seeking their partners, and the only way to help her heal is to remind her wolf I am the Alpha. The dominance with the energy tying us together will bring out her other half.

I unzip my pants, and my cock springs out. Her attention falls to my dick. There's hunger in her eyes as my scent twists with hers. She blinks, fear blooming in her irises, but she isn't pulling away anymore. I push my pants down my legs and step out of them before laying them alongside my shirt.

My hellcat looks at me, utterly lost.

"Now, show me, gorgeous. Show me how you touch yourself when you're alone and thinking of me. And don't fight me on this."

Her face pales, but her hand slips down her stomach and to the area between her legs. Then she pauses.

"No, no," I say. "That won't do. Open up."

"I know what you're doing. I will never submit to you!" She glares at me yet her body purrs for me.

"Then your wolf will never come out." I growl, needing her to stop fighting me.

She glares at me for the longest moment, and I don't back down. Her muscles tense as she gradually pries her legs wide, her hand cupping her pussy. At first, she just lies there, battling her own arousal. Then her fingers work slowly, sliding along the folds. Her pussy glistens with arousal, so pink and wet.

"Good girl."

I grow harder and harder at watching, so close to coming all over the bed.

A moan slips from her lips as she works her fingers, her legs falling wider apart. I'm on the verge of fucking off my self-control and rutting her like a wild animal.

Her heady smell fogs my head, and I'm on the bed before I even decide to move. I'm on hands and knees, my head lowering between her thighs, and I take a deep inhale, letting every cell in my body recognize and imprint her onto me.

I drag my lips along an inner thigh, her whimpers driving me crazy. She draws her hand back, offering herself to me, needing this as much as I do. I push her thighs wider still. My tongue slides out, and I lick the length of her soft flesh. She quivers under my touch, clutching a pillow and pressing it to her face.

I kiss her softly, teasing, sucking on her clit. I hold open her little pussy lips and drag my tongue over them, devouring her. Her body shakes, her hips rocking. Clasping on to her thighs, I eat her out and plunge my tongue into her liquid heat. She smells incredible.

She is mine to claim, to take over and over.

The primal hunger from my wolf rises through me so powerfully, he leaves me shuddering.

With a roar, I pull back and lift myself to my knees, staring down at my mate. She's the most beautiful thing I've ever seen.

I reach over and rip the pillow off her face.

"I want you to look at me as I fuck you and make you scream."

She stares at me with such fearful eyes that doubt creeps over my mind. I'm not someone who backs down when what I need to do will help someone, even if they don't see it themselves. I charge ahead and get things done. But with my little hellcat, I smell her sickness, and I remember the blood in the trashcan. She needs this so badly, but I can't push her.

"No, you're not really ready," I announce. As much as my chest splinters and my rock-hard cock hurts like a bitch, I pull back. "We can try this another time." I draw her legs closed and sit on the edge of the bed, looking away.

I scrub a hand over my moist mouth and chin, still drowning in her arousal, but I don't want her remembering me this way.

"Dušan," she whispers, her hand tenderly settling on my shoulder. "I'm just…" She clears her throat and I turn to face her. She's completely naked and kneeling behind me. "It's my first time. And"—she lowers her gaze—"I'm scared it's going to hurt." The vulnerability in her voice affects every inch of my body, sending a fierce surge through me.

I cup the side of her face and she leans into my touch. Looking into those heartfelt eyes, her ache is mine. I understand fear all too well. "It will hurt a little bit, but it will then hurt in an incredible way, I promise."

"I want you. I want your help. I don't want to die from my wolf. Please." Her fingers press into my arm with desperation. She isn't accepting defeat, but facing the truth.

A deep ache in my chest rattles, and I'm impressed that she has finally come to accept her situation. That my intention isn't to just bed her, but to help her. I stare at the pleading in her eyes, at her messy dark hair, at her erratic breathing. I feel the energy between us in my bones.

"I will take care of you. You are mine now, Meira."

Her eyes never leave mine. She clings on to me as she closes in and kisses me. Soft lips graze my mouth. She shivers against me. Her tenderness squeezes my heart. I still have to learn of her past. We all have darkness in our past, and I want to discover hers. I want to show her she's no longer alone. I want her to feel safe.

"I need you, Dušan," she says against my mouth.

"And you have me." I kiss her back, one hand to the back of her head, the other on her arm. She tastes like the sweetest cherries. We kiss until she's breathless, until I'm so lost, I forget how to breathe.

I guide her back onto the bed and she shuffles up, grinding into the mattress. I press my weight between her thighs and run my tongue down her neck, across her collarbone, tasting her salty skin. I take her nipple into my mouth, gently gnawing on it.

She writhes beneath me, her hips rocking back and forth, my cock sliding against her slickness.

She is so perfect moaning beneath me. Her body responds to my every touch. I collect the other breast into my mouth, taking my time, needing her desire to build back up, for her to be drunk with need.

The room swims in our scents. Her fingers dig into my arms, her groans grow louder. I stare at her beauty, and she holds my gaze as I slip my hand down between our bodies and rub her engorged clit. It drives her insane as she slides underneath me. Her little pussy so wet. She's ready, so I press the tip of my dick to her entrance, feeling her soaking wetness. She gasps a bit, and the sound is an addiction.

"I promise to go slow at first," I say. "I will never hurt what's mine. Are you mine?" I ask, more to hear her say the words than anything. I already know it to be true.

She holds on to my arms, her wolf whining in her chest. She is so fucking arousing. When her lips finally part, a primal groan spills out. And I know she's ready.

She wrenches her head forward to meet me in a kiss, and I push gradually into her soft core.

"I'm yours," she cries out.

She is so tight, and the need to explode inside her thunders through me. My cock aches as I stretch her wider until my tip hits a soft barrier, and I know what that is. I am her first. I pull out and slide back in quicker this time, but not all the way. I need her close to coming, so she experiences less pain.

With her head tipping back, her throat is open and exposed to me. I watch her bouncing breasts, the tightness of her stiff nipples.

"Make it hurt more," she demands, spreading herself wider. "Please."

Goddamn, she is going to be the end of me. I lose all control around her. I am burning up, desperate to let myself sink in all the way.

"You smell so fucking beautiful."

She digs her nails into my arm, and with each moan she unleashes, I push myself, I go deeper. I fuck her faster now and thrust right past the soft barrier, sliding all the way into her.

Her screams fill the room, her back arching, her walls clenching around me. I'm losing myself to her, but I draw it partially out, leaving just my tip inside her, eager to fill her over and over.

"Are you hurt?" I ask.

Her eyes flash open, her breaths racing. I love how red her cheeks glow. "More. Don't you dare stop."

"Fuck, Meira." I plunge back into her on a hard thrust, slapping into her.

She cries out as I hammer into her, pushing her, taking her, owning her.

Her scent curls around me like a blanket smothering me. And my wolf is right there, his energy intertwining with hers, roaring in my chest. He senses what belongs to us.

Her body thrums as I lower my hand to her pussy, my thumb pressing to her clit, rubbing it in small circles, building her orgasm.

"Come for me, beautiful," I say.

She screams louder, and my cock twitches, the base swelling, knotting. At that same moment, Meira convulses and screams, and I explode with my own orgasm. I pulse into her, pumping rivers of seed, filling her up. The longer my knot remains in place and holds the seed inside her, the higher the chance she'll be impregnated.

Gods, she is stunning in that moment of pure bliss. Her inner walls clench around my cock, squeezing and milking me.

I hiss. Warmth floods my cock as her slick coats me.

I'm drowning in her arousal. Her head is back once again, and in a moment of pure desire, I bare my teeth and sink them into the side of her exposed neck, drawing blood and tasting her orgasm in the air. I pull back from her neck, the coppery tang on my tongue.

Energy flares over my arms. Time fades, and I don't know how long we are entwined together.

Except there's no wolf pushing for release, and I can't stop the disappointment from slipping over my thoughts.

Meira's sexy moans are endless. Her brow is a sheen of sweat, and I want to remain buried in her for eternity. But I'm missing something about her wolf, something that isn't clear.

"I'll never let you go," I declare, the knot easing, and slowly, I draw out of her. I sit back on my heels and admire her beautiful pussy, at the seed and her cum dripping out.

"Stay there. I'll get you cleaned." I climb to my feet, my legs shaky and my head dizzy from the intensity.

"Dušan," she says.

I glance back at her over my shoulder. "Yeah?"

"You better not let me go," she growls.

CHAPTER 13

DUŠAN

It has been three sex-induced glorious days since I first claimed Meira. Her heat is explosive, and she's on me the moment I join her in my room. But there's still no sign of the wolf emerging. It should have done so by now. She's in heat, her body preparing for motherhood... but I have no idea if she can even carry children with her sickness—with the wolf still inside her.

Her scent still teases my nostrils. Sweet honey and roses, with a hint of cinnamon, which is her wolf. I recognize her smell anywhere now as it's blended into my senses. So are the sounds she makes with her arousal, which sing in my thoughts.

She affects me so much that now her absence seeps through me, a constant calling to my wolf.

I've marked her as my own, claimed her temporarily. Until her wolf unleashes, our connection will never be fully merged.

Bardhyl joins me in my office and slumps into the seat across from my desk. A new scratch down his cheek blushes red. "Found a girl, just barely. Fucking rogue wolves are desperate out there for a female. I had to fight two to get this girl. She's twenty and is coming into her heat. So it's perfect."

"You did fantastically. We need her in a quick mating ceremony in front of Alphas to make sure none of them are her fated mate before we send her to the X-Clan."

Bardhyl dusts his hands for show. "Done. She's ready to go."

I nod my head. "I'm impressed. Okay, arrange delivery in two days' time. She'll need a wash, feeding, new clothes, and the lowdown on where she's going." I reach into my top drawer to collect my tablet.

"On it. You're calling Ander?"

"Going to do this now, then Mad and Caspian can get their asses back home."

Bardhyl's upper lip curls into a sneer at their names.

I speak before he does. "I know what you're going to say, but Mad was appointed by our father before he passed."

"So? Fuck him and—"

"And what? Throw Mad out to the infected? You know I won't do that."

"Just so you know, if he does anything wrong on this trip to ruin our trading relationship, I'll put him in his place. I've had enough of his shit. You know before he left, the jerk changed all the locks on the sheds with a new password? It took us days to unlock them to reach our weapons."

I huff and shake my head. Mad is a prankster, but it doesn't make him malicious. He grew up with the same father as me, given the same beatings. We had different mothers, but they had no power over the previous Alpha of Ash Wolves. We all deal with the shit from our past differently.

I hit the call button on the video chat and sit back in my seat as Bardhyl leaves my office.

"Dušan." Ander greets me. His dark hair sits messily around his face. He's not wearing a shirt, and in the background is a kitchen. I must have caught him off guard.

"Ander," I answer, raking a hand through my hair. "I wanted to provide you with a brief update on the Omega. Is now a good time?" Tension flares across my shoulders that he won't accept a new girl over Meira.

A female's voice murmurs in the background of the video.

"No, stay," Ander insists, turning to look at someone at his side. "Please," he says softly.

The gentler side of Ander surprises me, as I've never seen him this way during any of our dealings. He's always in control, as any Alpha should be.

When he looks at me, I raise a brow out of pure understanding that only a female could soften an Alpha's heart. "Don't start," he mutters to me, then he refocuses on someone out of sight, stretching his arm out for them.

I can't help but grin at him, well aware that as much as Alphas try to hold these positions of power, we can all have our moments of weakness as well.

My gaze turns to a woman stepping into view. Her auburn hair, still wet, is draped over her shoulder. The dress she wears hangs loosely over her small frame. When she looks at me, all I see are blue piercing eyes. She's gorgeous.

"This is the Shadowlands' Sector Alpha," Ander says, drawing the woman into his lap. "Dušan, this is my Katriana."

It's good to see Ander has found his Omega. Seeing them together brings back memories of Meira and me last night. With it comes my rampant heart beating excitedly to visit her again, to take her to my bed every night until her wolf breaks free.

"Lovely to make your acquaintance, Katriana."

"You too," she replies, then she clears her throat. "Romania, right?"

"What used to be Romania, yes." I offer her a smile, and all I can picture is Meira, the urgency to go find her waiting in my room. "I'm sorry to interrupt you and your Alpha, but I promised him an update today."

"Indeed you did," Ander agrees, kissing Katriana's neck.

I avert my gaze as he finishes, letting my mind wander to the tenderness of Meira's skin under my lips. How I need to find a way to safely coax her wolf free so she can take her spot by my side. She is my mate, and now I need to help her. The longer her wolf remains at bay, the more worry churns in my gut. Survival for half-breeds is low... not impossible, but goddamn difficult. I drive those thoughts away, refusing to even entertain the possibility.

"What's the sensitivity level of our topic?" Ander asks, drawing my attention.

"Green." I understand right away he doesn't want his Omega to know all the details of our trade.

"Proceed," he murmurs, wrapping his arms around the Omega in his lap.

"We found your tenth promised wolf, but there's a complication. I need to switch out the product for a better fit." I study the Alpha for his reaction, not wanting this to ruin what we have set up.

He frowns. "What kind of complication?"

I stare at him for a long while, trying to work out the best way to explain without giving away too many details. Finally, I say, "A similar one to your current situation."

His eyebrows lift. "Oh." The way he intently looks at me, the corners of his eyes creasing, I can tell he understands. "Well, right then. A replacement is acceptable. How soon will you be transporting her?"

"Two days' time, unless you need her sooner?"

A quick shake of his head. "Two days is perfect. We have a social gathering planned that evening to introduce your wolves to my pack. Perhaps Mad and Caspian can stay for the festivities before returning to you?"

There is an eagerness in his voice, which tells me he's offering his hospitality as a confirmation he's content to keep trading more in the future. And this is exactly what I need. Maybe those two inviting themselves to stay with the X-Clan Wolves isn't completely a waste of time.

"They would be honored to stay," I say. "Thank you, Ander."

"You as well, Dušan."

"And nice to meet you, Katriana," I conclude in a softer tone before I hang up on the call.

Meira

I'm stir crazy closed up in Dušan's bedroom, and I miss him terribly. Despite it being days since I've seen Lucien, he's on my mind constantly as well. That kiss we experienced stays with me along with why he pulls away from me.

There's a guard at the door to stop me from sneaking out. Now I'm stuck in here with a desire that burns within me so wickedly, it never leaves me.

Dušan insists his bite mark and our sex makes me smell like a claimed female to other wolves for a few days only. Anticipation stretches inside me for his return.

Except worry is constantly coiling my chest. Why hasn't my wolf come out?

What if she never does? What if each time the sickness returns, it grows worse until it eventually kills me? I've never thrown up blood before. I know something is wrong—I feel it in my bones. So Dušan is right in trying to get my wolf out of me, to tame my human side that is carrying the sickness. Transformations heal any illnesses shifters may have contracted.

I turn and walk across the room before

crawling onto the bed, feeling so many emotions inside from fear to anger to a desperation to have my Alpha near me. His markings have opened something up between us.

The pillows and bedsheets carry Dušan's masculine, woodsy scent filled with pheromones. The smell of his seed and my arousal lingers too. An instinct jolts awake within me, and my core clenches with need. I shut my eyes and curl in on myself, wanting to drown myself in his smell. Slick pools between my thighs at the need that sweeps through me for Dušan.

There is no doubt now that he is my fated mate. My body and wolf yearn for him, cry out for him. My breaths spasm in my lungs, and a burning heat sweeps over me. For so long, I tried to ignore what I was—an Omega, a shifter ravenous to find my mate, a half-breed in deeper trouble than I ever thought.

Dušan's scent sinks through me, and I feel like I'm going to burst with the ache curling in my gut. I push myself out of bed, needing fresh air, anything to calm myself.

A knock comes at my door before it swings open.

The hairs on my nape bristle and I stand there, half-expecting Dušan.

Except it's Lucien who enters. His nostrils flare with a deep, shaky inhale, and something glints over his eyes. He can smell my desire, my need, and his Alpha's as well.

"I had to see you," he says, his voice deep and gravelly, as though he's struggling with his emotions. "I tried to stay away," he admits, the corners of his mouth pulling tight.

I can't hold back the smile on my face at seeing him, at how much I missed him. "I need some fresh air," I plead as I step closer.

He nods and stretches his hand out for me. I accept, and the moment our hands touch, that jolt of desire sparks to life just as it had over breakfast a few days ago.

Our gazes clash. He feels it too, just as he sensed the attraction between us when we first met.

His fingers curl around mine, and he leads me out into the hall quickly. The guard standing there just watches me and doesn't say a word.

Next thing I know, Lucien and I are running down the hallway, my wolf fueled with adrenaline —with the need to hunt. Lucien glances back at me, that hunger lashing over his face. I've never felt like this before.

I should be scared and ashamed at wanting to be with Lucien as my body craves Dušan. I've become an Omega who mated with the Alpha of the Ash Wolves but who can't control her instincts or reactions.

Turn back! I yell in my head, but my wolf takes charge. The longing comes off in waves, and my scent of fear coupling with it. Still, we don't stop. Not when we break out of the fortress, not when we rush into the dense woods within the settlement, and not when Lucien's clothes rip off his body as his body transforms.

Crisp air splashes over my face. I suck in breaths, watching with awe. His body elongates, his bones crack, his skin pops. Deep brown hair explodes over his wolf form. On four legs, he runs alongside me. He's huge, easily reaching my waist, and utterly stunning.

Electricity races up my spine.

My bare feet hit the ground. I don't feel the pebbles or twigs I tread on. Only the exhilaration thrumming through me, the power driving me. Is this how it feels to take the form of a wolf?

I drown in the intoxication of my wolf—the

primal instinct, the savagery, the familiarity. This is what I am meant to be. Free as a wolf, not hiding in trees and from my real form.

It hits me so hard...a feeling I've never experienced before.

When we finally reach the top of the hill where the metal fence blocks our path, we stop.

I gasp for air and collapse to my knees, half-laughing, half-trying to fill my lungs. "That's incredible. How could I have never felt this way before?"

Lucien in his wolf form curls around me, his gaze narrowing. I reach out gingerly and spear my fingers through his lush, thick coat. It's almost soft to the touch, and his skin is on fire.

He rubs himself across my back as he keeps circling me. My wolf surges in me. She's right there, whining for him, pressing against me for release. I sense her stronger now, like she's sliding right under my skin, desperate to tear out of me.

I breathe easy and open myself up as I did with Dušan last night. An ache comes with the concentration, and it burrows deep in my gut. I shut my eyes, squeezing them tightly. My heart hammers as sweat slides down my spine. Inside, I feel twisted and trapped.

A soft hand cups the side of my face, and I flutter my eyelashes open.

Lucien kneels in front of me naked, and all I can see is this big, powerful Alpha, a prime specimen that affects me. I drown in his woodsy, masculine scent. This beautiful man stares at me like he's inhaling me with his gaze.

"What's happening to me?" I swallow down a shaky breath.

"Your wolf is calling to mine... I can smell Dušan all over you, but I don't care. There's no jealousy, only the hunger to claim you as mine."

I blink at him. *His!*

I want to ask if he's toying with me, except I feel the sensation too. The intimate anticipation to reach over and kiss him just as I had wanted on our first kiss. My pulse races, because my body desires him while my brain tells me to push him away. To wipe that devious smirk off his face.

The inability to unleash my wolf plagues me—it scares me—but I don't know how I feel about being claimed by two Alphas. I'm struggling enough with Dušan's dominance and how my body melts around him—how my mind is not my own.

A cool breeze washes over us. My world spins

as my heart beats quickly. I try to fight it and bite down on my lip to hold back.

"You can't fight it," Lucien says, his voice heavy and deep. He reaches out for me, his hand clutching my skirt.

I can't breathe from our proximity. I'm so nervous about what this means for us…for me…for my wolf.

Rising to his feet, he towers over me. "I will take you," he says.

My voice won't work, words won't come, because I don't trust myself to say anything but *yes*. But my body gives him the response he seeks. My chest thrusts out as if I no longer control my body, my nipples pebbled tight, pushing against the fabric of my button-up dress.

He reaches over and grabs hold of the material over my chest, then rips it apart. Buttons flinging wildly in every direction like hail.

I flinch at his aggression, while heat pours through me at his dominance.

I'm wearing no underwear, since the last pair was torn to shreds by Dušan, so I'm utterly naked underneath.

Lucien's gaze falls down my naked body, over my breasts, to my stomach, then to the apex between my thighs. He makes a guttural sound that adds fuel to my heat.

Our mouths clash, fire exploding between us, and I'm lost.

"Take me," I urge, seduction filling every inch of me. "Please."

His tongue licks over my lips, strong hands running down my back and to my ass cheeks, prying them apart. We kiss hungrily. I wrap my arms around his neck, pushing myself closer. Heat melts at my core, and I feel the slick sliding down my inner thighs.

His mouth is on my neck, a large palm on my breasts, squeezing until it hurts. I growl and bare my teeth at the deepening heat.

A hand slides down between us and covers my sex. I moan, desperate for him to be inside me, to feel that thick shaft thrust within me.

Fingers glide over my heat. His mouth is on mine, his tongue pushing between my teeth, and I take all of him. He pushes two fingers into me, and I scream from the sexual spell that has gripped me.

"Please, Lucien, fuck me." The intensity is unbearable, my skin burns, my stomach tightens.

He grasps the back of my thighs and lifts me off my feet. Our scents are so strong, so potent. I wrap my legs around his hips and fling my arms tightly around his neck as I cling to him. He walks us toward a sloping part of the hill before he lowers himself to his knees with incredible strength. He places me on the ground, and I lie back as he spreads my legs wider. His gaze falls to the slick.

"Fucking beautiful and all mine." He dips down and without ceremony, cups his mouth over my shuddering core.

I moan, my back arching as he licks the length of me over and over, then plunges his tongue into me. My scream comes again from the tension building and building within me. I grip handfuls of grass as I ride his face, my hips rocking back and forth. A growl rumbles from my throat and into the air. It coils around us, binding us.

My muscles flex with the tension clenching in my gut.

"Come for me," he insists. The moment his mouth clasps over my folds and tugs on them, I lose it.

A storm rages through me as the orgasm claims me.

Lucien forces my legs wider. A sharpness sinks into the inside of my thigh, the pain flaming over me, clashing with the climax. Yet somehow, the feelings work together into the perfect sensation that owns me, caresses me, heats me, fulfills me.

"Open your eyes," he orders, his dominance cutting right through me.

I do as he asks and lift my gaze to his. He's staring at me with such devotion, such protectiveness. His chin and lips glisten from my slick, and a drop of blood rolls out from the corner of his mouth.

The fear sinks in.

"You marked me?" He imprinted himself on my skin, took my blood. How can we be bound in such a small time? So fast? I want to pull away and hide, while my body begs me to stay where I am, to throw myself at him.

He pushes himself between my legs. "Of course. Could you not feel our wolves are fated mates? I tried to fight it, but it was killing me to stay away from you for so long."

Before I can even make sense of his words, he slips the tip of his cock into me. I tense, already sensing his size.

"Let me in."

Breathing deeply, I adjust my hips to better accommodate his girth as I lose myself in his steel-gray eyes. They call to me and I let myself fall as he slides into me, filling and stretching me. He leans forward, his hands pressing into the ground on either side of my shoulders. He's huge, and there is something exhilarating about having a man so big claim me.

Liquid heat seeps from my core, which helps him drive into me faster. I curl my toes as he thrusts all the way in. I can barely breathe, his shaft filling me completely.

My heart slams against my chest as he draws in and out of me, faster and faster, the friction igniting a blaze between us.

"I will take you again and again—until you can't walk straight, until you realize how much you mean to me. How much you are meant to be with both of us... until we help bring your wolf out of you."

His words barely register as my body thrums with pleasure. I moan with each thrust, but I am under no illusion that somehow I've gained myself two fated mates. I've heard of men having multiple women, but not the other way around.

Lucien fucks me, ramming into me. I wriggle under him as a shudder rips over me.

My sex quivers, every cell in my body pulsing. He leans lower and brushes a tongue over my hard nipple, flicking it. I cry out, desire pooling in my stomach.

Then I feel him growing inside me.

I freeze as he stops thrusting into me, but he remains over me, meeting my gaze.

"You're knotting, aren't you?"

Still, my need has me heaving to get closer to him, bucking against him. Fresh slick slides out each time he shifts.

His eyes roll back into his head, a snarl pouring from his lips. His mouth twists, his body shivering with the intensity of what's coming. A growl rips from his throat.

And my ache eases to have him so swollen in me, the keening sound smothering me, digging into my flesh.

"You're so tight."

My soft inner walls pulse against his knotted cock, squeezing him.

He roars, his chest puffing out, his skin shining with a sheen of sweat. I adore the way he looks as he floats in euphoria. His lips settle over my nipple, and he takes me into his mouth, sucking hard. That same pleasure and pain swallows me. My own climax surges forward once again, building, tightening. Then it crashes over me so fast, my vision blurs.

The orgasm rips through me. "Lucien!"

He breaks into a ravenous growl, his hips moving ever so slightly as he pulses inside me. I feel the warmth, the streams mingled with my own climax. I shudder beneath him as he keeps coming. That's the thing about Alphas—they produce an insane amount of seed, filling me completely.

I float down from my euphoria, and an ache strikes me in the chest. It has nothing to do with my sickness or wolf, but the reminder that the reasons Alphas knot and produce so much is for the higher probably of impregnating their mates.

I stay still, Lucien still inside me. He watches me the whole time, but his thoughts are still trapped in his own orgasm, I see it in his eyes. He stays inside me until his knot eases enough to safely pull out.

After a while, he comes out of me completely.

I collapse onto the grass, my body sore and my heart racing. Slick and seed slip out of me, and there's nothing I can do about it right now. When I look over at Lucien, I see so much more than an Alpha who needs to follow his instinct.

He collects me into his arm and holds me against his strong chest. I grasp on to him, inhaling his scent, listening to his heartbeat pounding inside his chest. I should be embarrassed by being out here naked and having just had sex in the wild. But in Lucien's arms, I feel safe and protected. My head is still spinning, trying to make sense of my emotions and thoughts.

I look up at the healed scar over his collarbone.

"How do you feel?" he asks as he brushes loose strands from my brow.

"Like I've been hit by a tornado." I smirk and half-laugh. "But I don't understand. If I have now been marked by two Alphas, why hasn't my wolf tried to come out yet?"

He kisses the top of my head. "You've got to remember, your body has been accustomed to her staying inside you. It's clinging on."

A shudder of dread pulls at my nerves. "And what if she never emerges? Then I stay as I am. I've lived this all my life, and I'm fine."

I'm barely thinking straight as my body still hums from our sex. But if she won't come out, then I can live with that. The question is… will the Alphas?

"How long have you been sick?" he asks with authority in his voice.

I look down, but he lifts my chin to look at him. "Meira, how long?"

"My whole life," I whisper, as if saying it softly will hide the truth. "My wolf has been holding back the sickness."

"And have you always vomited blood?" His gaze holds mine.

I blink at him, my voice vanishing. "I don't want to talk about this," I rasp out. I wriggle to get out from under his hold. Pushing myself to my feet, I collect my torn dress and slip my arms through the sleeves before pulling it tight around my chest since its missing all its buttons. Warm slick rolls down between my legs, and I need to wash.

"Meira." He grasps my arm and forces me to face him. "If you're getting sicker, what happens when your human side completely gives out?"

My gaze lowers to my bare feet, and my heart splinters. I lift my head and hold myself strong, putting on a brave face because I'm terrified of dying. "My mama always told me not to be afraid of death. That it comes for all of us." My face blanches at the memory of losing her, and that maybe I won't be far behind.

I swallow hard and turn away from him, but he

catches my wrist and hauls me back to him. My hands jerk forward out of instinct and plaster against his solid chest.

His expression is furious, and his eyes look glazed over. "Do you know what happens when you die?" he barks, and I tremble in his grasp. "It's the people left behind like me who end up suffering, who pray for death every day. Fate can't fucking do that to me again."

Wait, what? *Again?*

CHAPTER 14

LUCIEN

"Whom did you lose?" Meira's tender words touch me more than she might ever imagine. Meira stands there, pulling her blue torn dress around her body and clutching the fabric at her chest.

She stares at me, waiting for my soppy story. We all have one in this godforsaken world. They call us survivors, but that's not what we are. We're the unlucky ones who get to see what it's like living in a rundown world that wants us dead.

"It's nothing. Don't worry about it. I shouldn't have said anything." I lick my lips and start picking up the loose buttons out of the greenery around us. I ripped her dress, so it's the least I can do.

"I lost my mother," she starts, her voice shaky.

"I was fourteen when they attacked the settlement. I was the only one to survive, so I know how it feels to be left behind."

When I stand and turn to her, she's right next to me, her eyes heartfelt and glinting in the sunlight. "My mama was all I had left in the world," she says. "And I was forced to live alone in the woods, every day finding a way to survive."

My throat tightens and my mouth goes dry.

"How are you still so nice and put together after all of that?" I ask. "I still have nightmares of the things I've seen. I still try to tell myself that things might be back to normal one day. That's how I try to survive, by lying to myself. Now you tell me that's not fucked up." I glance up to the sky, blinking hard. Cataline, my soulmate I'd lost to the infected, has stopped visiting my dreams, but the ache of being ripped in half has never left me. It reminds me that nothing is forever. That getting too close is a disaster waiting to happen. Maybe I was reckless and desperate, maybe too much time has passed to remember the ache I escaped so long ago.

I glance down at her hand on mine, at the thin healed scar from my inner wrist to my elbow.

She reaches out and her gentle finger finds my

forearm. It comes with a surge of adrenaline, of pheromones, of the raw, primal instinct that drives shifters.

I have my suspicions that she has no clue how deeply imbedded a mating is. How her life will revolve around her mate's, and even being too far from them will be painful.

"You can talk to me," she murmurs.

I slide my hand into hers, our fingers intertwined, and draw her into a walk. "That goes both ways, my little wolf. Now, how about we go get you washed up and then eat, because I could eat a horse. Then we can talk late into the night. How does that sound?"

She tosses me a cute sneer, like she doesn't believe we're going to talk all night, but maybe this is my chance to be open with my past. To get her to talk more about her sickness, as I suspect that might have something to do with why her wolf remains stuck.

"Well, is that a *yes* to my offer?" I ask, ignoring the part in my head that's telling me I ought to speak to Dušan sooner rather than later.

But when Meira pauses to look at me while standing under a fern tree and the wind rips open her dress, revealing her delicious naked body, my heart hammers in my chest.

I quickly grasp the material and pull it back over her perfect curved body and she holds it in place with her small hands.

"What would happen if everyone in this pack found a way to become immune to the undead?"

Her question takes me off guard.

"Like, you know… imagine everyone living freely with no fear of the infected," she says.

My thoughts go straight to the X-Clan who are immune to the infected.

She continues, "I'm thinking how many more lives could be saved. How going into the woods to hunt shouldn't be fraught with danger." She shrugs. "I don't know. I'm just thinking out loud. Stupid thoughts, really." I detect a hint of annoyance in her voice.

"You have a beautiful heart, Meira. And you want to know my honest thoughts?"

She nods eagerly, looking at me expectantly.

"If such an elixir existed, the battle over control of it would end in bloodshed."

She stiffens and her smile dissolves as she realizes how easily such power could lead wolves to war.

Shadows crowd under her eyes as she glances down and nods her head. "I'd like to think wolves are better than that, wouldn't you?"

The vicious fights I've seen between shifters for the single position of Alpha of a pack, the backstabbing in the hierarchy, the pain so many cause to get ahead is not indicative of a society who'd work in harmony. Under a strict rulership like Dušan's, it's possible, but it makes our fortress a target for every pack out there. We'd need a place that makes us untouchable.

"Maybe, and I really hope you're correct," I answer. "First, we need to find this cure, right? Let's head inside." We stroll through the woods within the settlement grounds, Meira staying especially quiet. I have so many things to ask her about her past, about things she likes, and we have time to get to know each other now.

Once indoors, we head downstairs and quickly reach the communal bathroom. Inside are two female Betas in the steaming water. They bow their heads at my arrival and continue chatting. I guide Meira to the showers at the back of the room and ensure that the room is empty first.

"I'll stay guard out here. There are fresh towels

in there. I'll get someone to bring you some clothes too."

She steps toward me and has a look on her face like she's about to ask me something. I might be misreading the signals, but the words spill from my lips. "You want me to join you?"

A half-chuckle is her response as she strolls inside and vanishes into a shower cubicle.

I glance her way and scratch my head. Is that a yes?

Dušan

"Ander," I answer the call as I sit in my leather chair at my desk.

The X-Clan Alpha doesn't greet me but just stares at me through video comm. He isn't alone as one of his own stands near. Something's wrong, and the tension in my stomach hardens.

"It's been brought to my attention that your Second and Caspian have taken twelve vials of my serum to create X-Clan Wolves," Ander finally says, surprisingly calm.

A chill shudders through me. "I'm going to fucking kill them!" I blurt out, regretting losing control so easily. I rein myself in and brace myself. Their actions punch me in my gut. I am going to murder Mad. I never should have trusted him. I should have demanded he return home the moment they made the delivery.

Thoughts rip over my mind about what Mad wants with the serum. Ander's team uses the serum to create X-Clan Wolves out of humans.

Shifting in my seat uncomfortably, I answer, "Ander, I know nothing about this, I swear on my life this was not coordinated under my leadership." A growl rumbles in my chest, my hands fisting at my side. "What Mad and Caspian have done has been of their own volition. I would never jeopardize our relationship this way."

His golden eyes pierce into me, and I square my shoulders.

"What benefit do I gain from stealing from you?" I point out as I realize that Mad must be searching for a way to make Ash Wolves immune to the infected since the X-Clan are unaffected. He must think the answer lays in this serum. We'd been talking about finding a remedy for years.

Sonofabitch! Why the fuck didn't he tell me first before pulling this stunt?

"I don't want to put a strain on our trading," Ander states. "And I do believe you weren't aware of their actions."

"I will personally deal with this issue quickly and return the serum to you. You have my word. I'm guessing the pair have already left your compound?"

My skin burns with fury.

He nods, and we continue talking about the severity of this situation and how to better secure our trading in the future. On the inside, I'm seething and ready to explode. Once I get a hold of those two, they will be lucky to breathe another day.

CHAPTER 15

BARDHYL

*S*weat trickles down my back the moment I walk into the bathroom. Steam curls up from the surface of the bath and the first thing my gaze lands on are two young Beta women in a corner of the bath chatting. Many use the place for destressing. They're facing each other, the water to their necks, and only when they look my way do they bow their heads.

There's no connection for me to Beta females. They aren't compatible with Alphas…it all comes down to knotting. Their bodies don't release the pheromone to trigger our knotting and swelling. A while ago, Dušan told me of a barbaric story of a Beta Ash Wolf female raped by group of Alphas. They'd trapped the woman's daughter in the room to arouse the Omega inside of her to allow the men to knot. Thing is, Betas aren't built for the knot the way an Omega is.

The poor woman died, and the daughter, Daciana, was a shadow of herself afterward. Dušan had no choice but to send her to X-Clan, because there was no way she would accept living with Ash Wolves after that horrific ordeal. Dušan butchered the Alphas with his bare hands when he found out. I would have done the same, but I'd have taken my time so they would have felt every excruciating ache.

From what I've heard, Daciana is quite satisfied with her new arrangement in Ander's pack now.

Stalking past the bath, I meet Lucien's gaze from across the room. He has his back pressed to the brick wall, but he straightens on my approach.

"You come to bathe with the women again?" he jokes and we hug with a clap to each other's backs.

"Maybe when the Omegas come to bathe, I'll return." I smirk and wink at him. Until Omegas find their mate, there's nothing stopping them from having a good time.

"So you tracked me down. Who's looking for me?" he asks.

"Hard not to track you down, bruh. I can smell

her all over you and the entire pack is talking about you fucking Dušan's Omega up in the woods."

"Fuck!" He rubs a hand over his mouth. "So I'm guessing Dušan's asked for me, then?"

I nod. "But go see Mariana first. She has Meira's blood results you requested. Mad was in her lab room too, going over the results. When I questioned him, he told me to go fuck myself."

Lucien stiffens. "That prick is back?" Lucien spits. "Does Dušan know?"

"Fuck no. The sneaky rat came in without telling anyone. I only saw him since I went to check on Mariana after her mother passed."

"Hell, shit's gonna explode, and Dušan is gonna be fuming." Lucien's shaking his head, fury lashing his face. The cords in his neck twitch, as does the nerve on his temple.

"Okay, you stay here and take Meira to her room once she's finished in the shower."

"You go. I'll take it from here," I say.

He gives me a nod and marches out of the bathroom. In truth, Dušan called Lucien about a conversation he had with the Alpha of X-Clan. I doubt our Alpha has even been out of his office or spoken to anyone this morning to hear the rampant rumors. In truth, I'm not surprised since the small encounter I had with Meira left me completely mesmerized. And I've done everything in my power to resist going back to her… clearly, Lucien failed.

Back in Denmark, it's common for females to have more than one mate. The question is more if Dušan is open to it because it's not common here.

Movement from the shower room draws my attention to the door opening as Meira steps out in clean clothes and a purple dress hanging off her arm. Her wet hair is pushed off her face. Black leggings hug her gorgeous toned legs, and a wrap-around blue top with a low V-neckline follows every curve of her sexy-as-hell tits.

I don't say anything, just waiting for her wandering gaze to meet mine.

"Hey, Angel Legs." My gaze drifts to the drop of water from her hair beading over her shoulders and rolling down the front of her cleavage.

The pulse in my neck jumps wildly, my groin aching.

"Last time I saw you, you pushed me into a house."

I raise a brow. "You fell inside after you kissed me."

The coloring in her cheeks reddens, and I enjoy watching her flush, wondering if she's that color when she's being fucked. The thought has my cock straining in my pants.

She lifts her chin high, her jawline tight. "Where's Lucien?"

"You're stuck with me, Cupcake. He had to go see Dušan."

Her eyes widen and she stiffens as her mouth parts, but the question never comes. I know exactly what she wants to ask, but her words never come.

"Come. I'll escort you to your bedroom."

She studies me, seeing right through me, then asks, "Maybe we can go sit outside for a bit? The inside feels stifling on such a nice day." I hear the fear in her voice.

"Of course," I say and take her purple dress, which I place in a corner basket for communal washing. Then, we stroll out of the bathroom and turn left down the hall. We walk past a couple, their whispers reaching us.

"She's with another man already?"

I shake my head at the gossip mill in this place.

"Dušan is very territorial, but he's also a

generous Alpha," I say to Meira who doesn't seem to notice the couple we pass.

"Why are you saying that to me? Is there something you want to tell me?" She fiddles with the tips of her long, brown hair.

"Is there something *you* want to tell me?"

She half-laughs when she looks at me, then as we reach an arched alcove, she turns on me rapidly. "You know, don't you? About me with Dušan and Lucien. I can see it in the grin you're trying to hide. So tell me... Is Dušan going to hurt Lucien? God, you must know something. You need to tell me." Her voice climbs.

Her panic drives my pulse, but I hold my hands up in a playful surrender and offer her a small smile. "Well, I know once a wolf connects with another wolf, it's for life. And I also know that until you have your first transformation, neither Alpha can truly mark you as theirs even if you are fated mates, or stop others from trying to mark you as their rut partner."

The hum of adrenaline sounds in my head, along with my wolf pressing for release. He sees so much in Meira... I had hoped that my earlier feelings were just a physical attraction. Except I've never felt such intensity shuddering through me.

Her breaths hitch, and she feels it too. She backs away, her eyes widening with shock.

In haste, she rushes past me, careful not to touch me. I take her side when we reach the rear entry to the fortress that leads into the woods in the settlement.

Before we turn in that direction, an earth-shattering scream cuts through the air.

Meira flinches and bumps into me. I clasp a tight arm around her waist, holding her near.

Then an explosion of shouts and what sounds like a stampede swallows every sound. My heart slams to the back of my throat, and two Beta males dart past the arched entrance in fright.

My adrenaline rages and I turn to Meira. "Run upstairs to your bedroom. Lock yourself in and don't leave."

She's trembling. "What's going on?"

"I'm about to find out. Now go!" I turn her by the shoulders and push her to the steps. She grasps the metal railing and rushes up, glancing back at me with fear in her eyes.

"I'll come back for you. Go!" I bellow.

She turns and races upward while I lunge outside to find out what the fuck is going on.

Meira

Panic pummels through my chest. I know this drill. I've seen it too many times, and the fear I'm feeling isn't for my life. It's for this pack, for the Alphas I can't resist.

I abruptly stop halfway up the stairs and turn around to find no sign of Bardhyl. He's gone.

Terrifying screams erupt from outside, along with shouting and that skin-crawling groan that I know too well. The sounds of utter pandemonium shatter my world.

I'm clinging to the railing, my legs shaking. I feel the blood drain from my face because we are meant to be safe in this pack. The lofty metal walls, the powerful Alphas, the guards with guns. They promised fucking security!

This can't be happening again...please, not again.

I need to move, but for those few moments, I'm paralyzed to the spot as I remember losing my mama, the massacre in the settlement, and all those bodies.

My heart clenches with excruciating pain, my

eyes welling with tears as every thread of grief I've been holding on to rips me apart.

All I can picture is Mama on the ground, blood pouring from the deep gash across her torn throat. My cheeks are soaking from hot tears, and I wipe them angrily away with my fingers.

Swift and silent.

But I won't hide.

I'm running back down the stairs before I can stop myself and dart outside. The woods within the settlement are right at the doorway.

Shifters are scrambling for their lives amid the trees, wolves in animal form, and the settlement fence on my left is smashed open, as if something has driven through it.

The undead pour into the settlement with such speed, it leaves me dizzy—nothing stops the infected. Torn clothes, broken skin, mortal wounds, missing body parts—nothing stops the infected.

Ice cuts through me, and I can barely draw a breath. My hands tremble as I clasp my stomach, fisting the fabric of my shirt, twisting it with pure terror.

A woman falls to her knees in front of me, a lanky undead lunging for her.

My heart stammers, and instinct kicks in. I rush forward and snatch a branch from the ground, then swing it wildly at the creature's face before it gets a chance to bite her.

The thing jerks backward, giving the woman time to scramble out of there. For good measure, I slam the stick into the creature's face over and over before I jam the pointy end into his face, piercing the eye and driving the wood into its brain. It makes a splattering sound as the Shadow Monster silences and collapses. I stagger backward from the finally truly dead creature, swallowing past the boulder in my throat.

I sprint deeper into the forest, helping anyone I see in trouble the best way I can—with stones to smash in the undeads' heads, branches—anything to fight this battle.

An ear-splitting howl splinters the air, and I flinch around to find Bardhyl ripping his shirt off, his body already transforming into the biggest wolf I've ever seen. With a white pelt and black-tipped ears, he is stunning as he lifts his head and unleashes a howl.

A man with a gangrene arm and no lips charges up behind him, but Bardhyl snaps around in a heartbeat and swipes his massive paw at the monster, shredding its chest down to the bone. Another swipe, and his head is ripped right off. The headless creature crumbles and twitches, half its ribcage sticking out and broken.

Another Shadow Monster, with the contents of its stomach trailing behind him, lunges toward the Alpha. I'm going to be sick, but I still dart forward to intercept the attack, shoving my hands into the bony chest just as it reaches for Bardhyl. I knock it to the ground with my momentum and smash the rock in my hand into his head, over and over, blood and innards spilling free.

I scramble off it, feeling sick to my stomach from the sight, and suck in harsh breaths. Bardhyl brushes past me, his eyes narrowing and there is acceptance in his gaze, the need to attack our enemy. Then he lunges toward a horde of undead coming.

I don't waste a moment and rush toward the gap in the fence, needing to somehow stop more from coming in.

I shove past the undead and dart around the trees, past shifters fighting.

The twisted and warped fence is bent forward, clearly driven down by a vehicle.

Someone snatches my wrist and jerks me

toward them aggressively, my heart blazing at the movement.

I grip the blood-stained rock over my head as I stumble to find my feet, then come face to face with the white-haired Alpha from the aircraft I'd escaped weeks before.

A gasp falls from my lips. "Mad!"

What's he doing here?

He whacks the back of my hand, and my stone flings out of my grasp. "So Dušan found you after all." He sniffs the air, then grins, sensing the Alphas' scents on me. "You haven't wasted your time, have you, bitch?"

I slam my fist into his chest, then slash my free hand at his face, nails scratching the side of his cheek, breaking skin.

Fury twists his expression into one of pure ugliness as his fist swings, then clips the side of my face.

My legs give out and I drop to the ground, my face an explosion of pain that ripples over my skull. Holding the injured side of my head, I cry from the agony.

He grabs my hair, then hauls me to my feet, and I tug back on my hair to stop the pain. Tears thread down my face. Fisting my hair, he tilts my head back violently, his face in mine. Ice-blue eyes slice right through me with venom.

"I know what's in your blood, why the infected don't touch you. Your blood tests show it all." He spits the words at me. "But I can't have you ruin my plans, Meira. I can't have you ruin them at all."

He seizes my jaw with his hand and squeezes. I whimper from the pain, from the fear of what this Alpha will do to me. The greedy look in his eyes is the reason I don't want anyone to find out the truth. Why I tell no one that I'm immune to the undead.

Someone slams into my back, and I'm shoved against Mad. In that sliver of a moment, his grip slips. I drive my hands into his chest and send him reeling backward.

Pivoting on my heels, I catapult myself into the river of undead at my back. Spinning back, Mad rises from the ground, his eyes spewing hatred, his hands fisted, but as the infected turn toward him, he retreats and runs.

The need to escape pounds in my head. I'll never be safe here, not with wolves like him, who see me as an opportunity once they uncover my secret.

Lucien's words spear over my thoughts. *If such*

an elixir existed, the battle to control it would end in bloodshed. He was right. Wolves will kill to get to me...

I curse myself and whack a palm into the side of my head. *Stupid. Stupid. Stupid.*

Why did I let myself think this place might be different? Why did I get close to the Alphas?

My feet already recoil toward the broken fence behind me. My heart is shattering slowly.

These undead, the cause of the horrific state of the world, brush past me, unknowingly saving me.

I lift my gaze to the battle, only to find Dušan and Lucien staring right at me from the fortress doorway. They can see me swimming amidst the enemy without being attacked.

An army of undead swarms between us, more pouring into the settlement, shoving past me.

And the Alphas see it all now. They see me, my real secret. The one thing that promises to make me a lab experiment.

Adrenaline pumps through my veins, and a sick feeling dulls my thoughts.

I can't be here. I can't bring war to their home.

My heart splinters into a thousand pieces between escaping so their pack doesn't go to war and staying to help them save the settlement.

My throat thickens, already longing for the connection I have with the Alphas. I crave the intimacy. Adore that Dušan did his best to protect me. My head sways in two directions.

I shudder when I spy Mad from a balcony in the fortress watching me... he's a cancerous leech, and I know he will do everything to destroy me, even if it means eliminating the pack.

I straighten my spine and turn on my heels before running out of the settlement. This is what I should have done the moment I arrived here.

"Meira!" Dušan's voice fades behind me.

I can't stay here. I can't risk them losing everything. The Alphas are strong. They'll fight with claws and teeth.

The pain of leaving them behind squeezes my heart, but I don't stop running away. I never will.

Swift and silent.

Dušan

She's gone, and all I see before she goes is the fear in her eyes. The infected moved past her like she didn't exist. I lunge forward, but Lucien grabs my arm and stops me.

"Dušan, I have Meira's blood test results from when I arranged from the sample I took when she first arrived." Lucien chokes on his words.

"And?" I snap, unable to stop staring out into the woods. Except I need my head screwed on straight. "I have to fight for my wolves. This can wait." But I can't lose Meira. My breaths stumble inside me.

"Fuck, just listen to me for a second." He sucks in a deep breath. "Meira has leukemia. And it's spreading through her human form. Mariana says the sickness mingled with her wolf side is what makes her immune to the infected."

I shake my head, trying to hear his words as I turn to my Third. I smell her all over him, and I clench my fists. But I can't see clearly through my fury.

"So, what is it then? Her sick blood is immune to the undead? She's the cure everyone dreams about and can help all our pack? A solution that will bring war to our doorsteps when everyone finds out?"

"Yes. But there's a problem."

I swallow hard and growl. "What could possibly be worse?"

"The leukemia is spreading fast through her human side, and she doesn't have long before her body dies. Then her beast will rip out of her body." He stares at me, and we're both thinking the same thing before he mouths it. "There'll be nothing left of her."

My heart cleaves in half, and the world fades around me. Every emotion hits me at once—anger, frustration, fear, and heartache. They grip me, shredding my insides as everything Lucien said plays out in my head. The mess this will turn into, coupled with Mad's return and the coincidental breach of our fence, makes my blood boil.

"How long does she have?" I tighten my fists, my knuckles turning white.

"A week or two at most, Mariana thinks. I'm surprised she's survived this long." His words are strained.

Silence falls between us. All I can think about is the longing in my heart, the sharp ache that reminds me that she's meant to be one of us.

And she ran because she knew we found out her secret.

Sweet fuck, Meira. Why run? No secret could make us want you any less.

"Sonofabitch!" A howl tears from my throat. "Lucien, let's kill every motherfucking infected. Then, we're claiming our mate."

Lucien's eyes widen in surprise, then he nods. "We're in this together."

A terrifying scream rings in the air, and we both snap toward the sound. In front of us, the sheer number of undead is terrifying… I have never seen this many near our settlement. Wolves are running in every direction. Chaos strangles our home.

Shivers ripple up my spine, and I pray to the moon that we'll live to see another day. With one look at Lucien, we both lunge into battle.

THANK YOU

Thank you for reading Shadowlands Sector, One

Reviews are super important to authors as it helps other reader make better decisions on books they will read. So if you have a moment, please do leave a review on Amazon.

Start reading Shadowlands Sector, Two today!

ABOUT MILA YOUNG

Best-selling author, Mila Young tackles everything with the zeal and bravado of the fairytale heroes she grew up reading about. She slays monsters, real and imaginary, like there's no tomorrow. By day she rocks a keyboard as a marketing extraordinaire. At night she battles with her mighty pen-sword, creating fairytale retellings, and sexy ever after tales. In her spare time, she loves pretending she's a mighty warrior, walks on the beach with her dogs, cuddling up with her cats, and devouring every fantasy tale she can.

For more information...
milayoungarc@gmail.com

Join my Wicked Readers Group

facebook.com/groups/milayoungwickedreaders

Manufactured by Amazon.ca
Bolton, ON